THREE

THREE

D. A. Mishani

Translated by Jessica Cohen

riverrun

First published in Hebrew in Israel in 2018 by Achuzat Bayit
First published in Great Britain in 2020 by

riverrun
An imprint of

Quercus Editions Limited
Carmelite House
50 Victoria Embankment
London EC4Y 0DZ

An Hachette UK company

A CIP catalogue record for this book is available from the British Library

Hardback 978 1 52940 009 0
Trade paperback 978 1 52940 008 3
Ebook 978 1 52940 010 6

10 9 8 7 6 5 4 3 2 1

Typeset by CC Book Production
Printed and bound in Great Britain by Clays Ltd, Elcograf S.p.A.

Papers used by Quercus are from well-managed forests and other responsible sources.

For Sarah Mishani, my father's mother,
and for Sarah Mishani, my daughter

'For the Son of man shall be delivered into the hands of men.'

(Luke 9:44)

'For the Son of man is not come to destroy men's lives, but to save them.'

(Luke 9:56)

One

I

THEY MET ON A dating site for divorced singles. His profile was unexciting, which was exactly why she wrote to him. Forty-two years old, divorced once, lives in a Tel Aviv suburb. Not 'excited to swallow life whole' or 'on a self-discovery journey I'd like you to join me on'. Two kids, five foot eight, college-educated, self-employed, financially stable. Political opinions: none. Some other items were left incomplete too. Three pictures, one old and two that seemed slightly newer, all of which showed something reassuring about his face, nothing too special. He was not overweight.

Eran, her son, had started therapy, and his therapist said it would be good for Eran to see that she was not just grieving, but starting to move on with her life. She tried to get the two of them back into a routine: supper at seven, shower, one TV show, and then they both got their bags ready for the morning. At half past eight or quarter to nine Eran would be in bed and she'd read him a story, even though he could read on his own, because it wasn't a good time to stop. After that she'd sit at the computer desk in the corner of the living room, reviewing profiles and reading messages, even though she knew she wasn't going to write back to any man who contacted her. She preferred initiating contact herself. It was late March, but in the evening she wore a jumper, and sometimes it was raining lightly when she got into bed alone.

She sent him a message – 'I'd be happy to get to know you' – and he answered two days later: 'Let's do it. How?'

They had an online chat.

'What school do you teach at? Primary? Secondary?'

'Secondary.'

'Can you say which one?'

'I'd rather not give details for now. It's in Holon.'

She was cautious, he was revealing. The items left blank on his profile were filled out as their conversations progressed. He liked to ride his bike. Mostly on Saturdays, in Yarkon Park. 'After neglecting my body for years, I've started going to the gym too. Delightful.' She didn't think you could tell from the pictures. He was a lawyer – 'Not one of those sharks, just an independent lawyer, with my own little firm' – and most of his work involved verifying eligibility and submitting applications for Polish, Romanian and Bulgarian citizenship for Israelis with roots in those countries. He got into the field after working for a few years in the legal department of an employment agency that brought foreign workers to Israel from Eastern Europe, and that's how he built up contacts in the various departments of interiors. 'Would you happen to need a Polish passport?' he asked, and she wrote back: 'No chance, my parents are from Libya. Do you have contacts with Gaddafi?'

Her friends at the school warned her against internet chats. They said you couldn't believe what people said about themselves. But he didn't say anything unusual about himself. On the contrary: it was as if he were trying to sound ordinary. After corresponding for a few days he asked, 'Are we going to meet eventually?' and Orna wrote, 'Yes, eventually.'

THURSDAY EVENING, HALF PAST nine. Early April.

He said she should decide where to meet, and she chose a café by Ha'Bima Square in central Tel Aviv. Three days earlier she'd met with Eran's therapist and had mostly talked about herself. The therapist had hinted that Orna might want to get some therapy too, and she'd laughed. She'd apologized for talking too much and explained that she couldn't afford therapy. She was only able to pay for Eran's sessions thanks to her mum.

The therapist advised her not to keep her first date a secret, but also not to make a big deal out of it. It was best not to ask her mum to babysit or have Eran sleep over with her, because she'd be more anxious than the two of them and would tell Eran more than he should know. She should try to get the same babysitter they'd used when Mum and Dad used to go out together. If Eran asked who she was going out with, Orna could say, 'A friend.' If he asked who the friend was, she could say he was a new friend whom Eran didn't know yet. His name was Gil.

Tel Aviv was crowded. The traffic jams started at the Shalom exit from Ayalon Highway and continued along Ibn Gavirol Street, and the new underground car park they'd built at the cultural centre was full. Gil had sent her his phone number that morning on chat, and she texted him to say she was running late. She drove back to the car park on Kaplan Street, left her car there and walked to Ha'Bima Square alongside groups of partiers, men with tattoos and beards, pretty girls and young couples with babies. Maybe she should have suggested a different place. Her outfit – white cropped trousers, matching white blouse, thin white jacket – made her feel old, or worse: like an old woman trying to look young. But the first thing Gil said helped her feel less alien:

'What are we actually doing here? I feel so old.'

It was much stranger than she'd expected, to suddenly start going out with men.

When she got there he stood up and shook her hand as though they were at a business meeting. He ordered a latte, so instead of wine she got non-alcoholic hot cider with a cinnamon stick. He wasn't thin, but you could tell he worked out. And he was dressed more casually than she was: jeans, blue shirt, white trainers. He took upon himself the role of the more experienced party, because he'd been on quite a few of these dates.

'Usually you talk about the divorce,' he said, 'swap war stories.

A bit like in reserve duty. It's pretty depressing but I'm willing to go first.'

She said, 'No, anything but that,' but she was curious to hear. Talking about it herself was out of the question; everything was still bleeding and unprocessed, sometimes not real at all. Even while she was on the date, she sometimes had the feeling that all this was not happening and that it was Ronen sitting there with her. Gil said he had two daughters, both in secondary school: Noa and Hadass. His ex-wife had initiated the divorce, and at first he'd resisted, probably not out of love but out of fear.

Unlike what had happened between her and Ronen, Gil and his wife had had a lengthy separation process. When his wife brought up the idea, he'd managed to persuade her to try to repair the relationship. Then there was a brief period of marriage therapy, and in the end he acquiesced. To the best of his knowledge she hadn't cheated on him, and she didn't have a boyfriend now either. She'd just stopped loving him, she'd lost interest, wanted to try something new, not give up on life, all sorts of things that he hadn't understood at the time, or hadn't wanted to understand; but today he understood more. All in all the change had made everyone's lives better. The girls' too. The divorce was easy, perhaps because they were both lawyers and money wasn't tight. His ex-wife stayed in their flat in Givatayim, and with the money they got from the sale of a rental flat they owned in Haifa, he bought a four-room flat not far away. He was recounting all this not for the first time, that much was clear, and his tone was so mollified that it made Orna feel just how wounded she was. Precisely because she thought her and Ronen's story was so different – but perhaps it wasn't? The lines Gil had said drily – 'Try something new,' 'Not give up on life' – exploded inside her like little grenades.

Gil didn't see any of this, or at least she hoped he didn't. When he asked, 'And how was it for you?' Orna said, 'Different. I have— We have a nine-year-old boy, and he took it really hard. But I'd rather not talk about that now.'

After that she wasn't there any more. Gil talked about his work, told her about quick business trips to Warsaw and Bucharest, tried to take an interest in her life and did not press her when she resisted. Time passed slowly. Ha'Bima Square filled up at quarter past ten, when the plays ended, and then emptied out. At twenty to eleven Gil ordered a Coke Zero and asked if she wanted something to eat, but she didn't even get another cider because she was hoping the date would end.

A little after eleven he said, 'Shall we?' and she said, 'Yes, we should, it's really late.'

'I'd be up for keeping our chat going, if you feel like it. And you also have my number,' he said by way of goodbye.

She wanted to phone the babysitter on her way to the car to ask if Eran was asleep yet, but she couldn't because she felt she might burst into tears.

2

A WEEK LATER, SHE SENT him a message.

'Gil, are you still there?'

'You mean here? Apparently for ever.'

She apologized for their date, explaining that she probably wasn't ready yet. He must have had a dismal time with her.

He wrote back: 'Not at all. And I completely understand because I've been there myself. No hard feelings at all. Maybe some other time.'

AT SCHOOL IT WAS end of term, and in the evenings she had exams to mark. She finished reading Eran *The Prince and the Pauper* and started *The Last of the Mohicans*, precisely because they were stories that had nothing to do with anything in their lives; they weren't about a boy coping with divorce but tales of distant times and places. She started tutoring pupils from other schools in the afternoons, so she wouldn't have to ask her mother for money beyond what she already borrowed for Eran's therapy. She gave four to six tutoring sessions a week and charged a hundred shekels an hour, which could amount to two thousand shekels a month, in cash. In summer the tutoring would end, but she'd signed up to mark matriculation exams so she'd have another source of income.

Friends from school, especially those who weren't close to her, tried to find out if she was ready to be set up. Quite a few men in their circles were starting their second rounds, and although most of them were the dregs, there were a few real catches. Orna rejected the offers. There were no more than a couple of new profiles a week on the site, and she kept coming across the same faces and the same lines trying to conceal the loneliness behind pretty words: 'Unwilling to compromise on anything less than true love', 'Looking for a partner for my life's journey', 'An unconventional man, the real deal, no lies and no masks'. They were all phoney, or not thin enough, or too young, aged twenty-eight or thirty, and Orna couldn't understand what they were doing there, just as she wasn't sure why she herself flipped through the site every few days without any real intention. When she wrote to Gil to suggest they go on another date, it was not really premeditated, just a spur-of-the-moment decision, although the thought had crossed her mind a few times.

He answered in a few hours: 'Happy to, but only if it's not out of pity.'

Orna sent a smiley face, followed by: 'Is self-pity okay?'

*

PASSOVER CAME AND WENT. It was a sad Seder, the first after the divorce. Just her and Eran, her mother, and her brother and his family at their home in Karkur. As always, far too much food and unintentionally painful conversation. No one mentioned Ronen. Eran clung to her the whole evening, didn't play with his cousins or join in to search for the Afikoman. The next day, on the holiday morning, she woke up a few minutes before six. The sky was heavy with rainclouds and it was unexpectedly cold. Their winter clothes were already stored on the top shelves of the wardrobe. She had no idea how they would get through the whole school holiday.

The babysitter was busy with school exams, so she was only free on Tuesday, but that worked for Orna. A quiet evening, with fewer partiers on the street. Gil wrote, 'I have another date on Tuesday, but if it's the only day you can do next week, I'll cancel.' Instead of making her happy, his honesty disgusted her, and she thought of backing out. I'm on the meat market, she thought. I'm part of the meat market.

Maybe there was no way around it.

'Can we not meet in Tel Aviv this time?' she asked, and he replied, 'Of course. Wherever you'd like. Yafo? Givatayim? The marina in Herzliya?'

'Isn't Givatayim too close for you?' She thought about his grown daughters, who might walk by the café. About his ex-wife.

'Very close. But honestly, I don't mind where we meet. They've opened some nice places near me on Katznelson Street, but I can get anywhere.'

SHE DIDN'T FEEL ANXIOUS before the second time, and that was strange. As if she were going to have coffee with a friend from work, or as if Gil really were 'a friend', as she told Eran.

She dressed casually and put on hardly any make-up, perhaps to send him the message that she wasn't playing by the usual meat-market rules. He wore athletic clothes again, with the same jeans and the same white trainers, but this time a white shirt. She thought he looked slightly thinner, while most men in Israel gained weight on Passover. They kissed on the cheek when she walked into the café, late again because she'd had trouble finding parking, and the kiss was friendly, befitting a couple who'd met more than twice. Gil smelled of a cologne she didn't recognize and immediately liked. A very sweet, chocolatey aroma, which one couldn't help wanting to smell again.

She tried to be less melancholy this time, more talkative, mostly after it occurred to her that Gil might regret giving up his other date for her. Still, she stuck to the role of the interviewer who doesn't say much about herself – and Gil agreed to be interviewed again.

'So, do you go on a lot of these dates?' she asked, and he answered, 'Fewer than I used to, but yes, quite a lot. I don't have much else to do in the evenings.'

'And nothing ever comes of it?'

'Usually not.'

Most of the time, he said, the women didn't write or call after the first date. A few did try to keep things going but he ignored them. Only rarely did it progress to a second date, and there'd been a total of three times when it had gone beyond that. Three times in over two years. That depressed Orna briefly, as though what Gil was saying offered a glimpse into her own future, but she perked herself up. Less melancholy, more talkative. This time she wasn't sinking. She felt able to be more relaxed and happy, maybe in part because she'd ordered alcoholic cider this time. The café, which Gil said he often went to in the mornings on his way to the office, was full of young people again, but this time it didn't bother Orna as much, and even helped. As did the fact that Gil had some red wine.

'Went beyond that – you mean sex?' she asked, surprised by her own brashness.

Gil smiled. 'Sex too. It evolved into something that lasted more than two or three dates, to a sort of beginning of something posing as a relationship.'

'And why didn't it work out?'

'I guess they didn't fall in love with me and I didn't fall in love either, and somehow nothing happened. It faded.'

He tried to avoid talking about the divorce, maybe because he sensed that was what had ruined their last date, but Orna was more confident now in her ability to tolerate the memories, which did indeed come up when he started to talk. She insisted on asking him about his ex-wife and daughters, to prove that she could, that something in her really was getting stronger, as Eran's therapist said it would, even if she couldn't completely feel it herself yet.

After the cider she ordered a glass of Merlot, and then Gil got another glass of wine, even though he'd finished his first one long ago – as if he'd been awaiting confirmation that she wasn't about to flee, that it wasn't presumptuous of him to order a second glass. On the way home in the car, she thought that what she liked about him on this date might not have actually been about him, but about picking up where they'd left off last time. By now she recognized the way he lowered his voice when he asked a question he feared might be too personal, the way he ran his fingers through his fair hair and smiled before he answered a question he found embarrassing, the disappointment in his eyes when he thought something he'd said had pained her and made her shut down, and his joy when he talked about his girls, Noa and Hadass.

His divorce agreement had given them shared custody, but he'd felt from the start that it wasn't easy for the girls, that they preferred to spend the week in the home they'd grown up in, in their own rooms, and so he didn't insist, even though he'd put a lot of money into their new rooms. At some point he gave each of the girls their own key to his flat and told them to come whenever they wanted to, without asking first or knocking. In the first three months they hardly came, and always texted him first, but it had gradually changed. He would come home from work in the early evening and find them in his kitchen or living room, doing homework or watching TV. Mostly it was Noa, the older one. His flat was less than a ten-minute walk from their house. His ex-wife didn't mind, and one could say that his home had become their refuge, or perhaps a place where they could practise what it would be like to have their own home one day. They came three or four times a week now, studied for their exams undisturbed, cooked dinner, tidied up on their own, and two weeks ago there'd been another important development: Noa had a boyfriend, and she'd asked him to sleep over for the first time, not at his ex-wife's but in her new room at Gil's place. She'd be seventeen in a month, and he and his ex were considering buying her a car together. He would pay for most of it because, after all, his finances were much more stable.

That was the only moment on the second date when Orna thought about Ronen and Eran. How different everything was with them. And for a moment she feared that her attempt to trap the despair and sorrow wouldn't succeed and they would be visible on her face like smudged make-up. She reminded herself of what Eran's therapist had said: Don't pressure him, Orna, give the boy time. He's on his way to overcoming the crisis, just like you are, even though you can't see it yet.

This date went by quickly.

It was after midnight when they said goodbye because she had to get home. For some reason they didn't kiss this time, even though at the moment of separation she wanted to smell Gil's chocolatey cologne again.

That night, a little before one, he sent her a text message: 'It was fun, Orna. Thanks.' And she responded, 'Thank you.'

3

WHAT SURPRISED HER WAS how patient he was.

At first she thought it was because he was going out with other women, but Gil said that after their second date he'd decided not to meet anyone else, so as to give it a real chance. He didn't suspend his online profile or remove it, but she didn't say anything about it so he wouldn't think she was spying on him – or so he wouldn't know that she was also still checking the site, without any real purpose, scanning new profiles as if she might be missing out on something.

MAY. SPRING.

After one more date in April, in May they see each other three times.

At school it's a busy time because of the upcoming matriculation exams. At home, Eran is talking about his birthday next month. Two hours before one of her dates with Gil the babysitter calls to say she can't make it because she has a temperature, and Orna is about to phone Gil to cancel, but she changes her mind – she is desperate to get out, having spent days rushing from home to school and back again – so she asks her mother to watch Eran. She takes into account the fact that her mother will ask questions, and she does. Orna says she's going out with Sophie, her good friend whom her mother knows well, but she puts on a smart, short dress, which surely makes her mother realize she's lying.

She isn't telling anyone about Gil for now, except Eran's therapist, because there's nothing to tell yet – she isn't in love with Gil and there's little going on between them – but perhaps also out of a conviction that if she doesn't tell, something will happen. She once heard an author on TV explain why she never showed anyone what she was working on: when something is simmering, you have to keep the pot covered.

They still haven't had any physical contact, apart from the occasional flutter of lips over cheeks. Is Gil dating other women after all? Most of the time she feels she is shutting herself off to certain thoughts and feelings and simply functioning, and that the dates with Gil are part of the attempt to function, to keep up the appearance of an ordinary life.

She wakes up in the morning to get herself and Eran ready for work and school, whispers, 'Good morning, Erani,' and smiles while she strokes his black hair and watches him open his eyes. She teaches the usual material, prepares her students for their Hebrew grammar exam, helps Eran with his homework in the afternoons, tutors to make some extra money, and usually manages to cook something for supper. Every so often she goes out with this guy she met. Everything is fine. Nothing is broken. She and Gil have pretty similar tastes in food and movies, he doesn't say anything that makes her feel embarrassed or ashamed about going out with him, he's good-looking, she likes being seen with him on the street, his Hebrew is better than average, sometimes even higher and more correct than hers, he's patient and courteous. In short, life goes on. She's not falling apart.

But at other times the unhappiness, or the hopefulness, disrupt her efforts to feel that everything in her life is normal, and she is overcome with dread when she thinks about the fact that she is going out with a man who is not Ronen, and that these are the things she consoles herself with – that they both like sushi, that he's not fat – as though within the course of a few weeks she has become a different woman, a much older one than she used to be.

Eran's therapist promises her that beneath the surface, which she usually experiences as a total collapse, time is weaving together a new order, a new life. But Orna cannot feel for more than a few moments at a time that what he says is right.

ON THE EVENING HER mother comes to babysit Eran, they go to a movie for the first time. *Interstellar*, at the mall. Orna is moved by the relationship between the father and daughter and can't stop crying when the movie is over, because of Eran and Ronen. Afterwards they go to a Japanese restaurant and she tells Gil for the first time about Eran and Ronen.

Eran is a special child, she explains. Introverted and very vulnerable. He's turning nine at the beginning of June. He's a little short for his age, thin and extremely shy, with almost no friends. The nicest thing that's happened to him recently is that he's discovering that he has a sense of humour, and he uses it a lot. He tries to make people laugh, mostly her, and is overjoyed when he manages to. In class he isn't brave enough yet. He is fascinated by aircraft – model aeroplanes, unmanned aircraft, drones, anything that flies. Lately he's also discovered cars and has started to collect little models, mostly ones her mum buys him. He was always very close to Ronen, even though Ronen travelled for long periods of time. He was an overseas tour guide – actually, he still is, but now he lives in Nepal. And he hasn't seen Eran even once since he came to Israel to sign the divorce papers in December.

For a second it seemed to Orna that Gil was about to put his hand on hers, which was on the table, and she hoped he wouldn't do it at that precise moment. He hardly asked any questions because he realized how sensitive the topic was, and Orna told him what she could:

That Ronen had married a German woman named Ruth, who was three years older than him and had four kids, and that they lived in Kathmandu, where they ran a hostel. Ruth was pregnant.

That Ronen had promised not to cut ties and to come and visit Eran often, but he hadn't come yet.

That they hadn't even Skyped since the end of February.

'Doesn't Eran ask about him? Does he talk to you about it?'

'Not to me. It's as if he never had a dad. But he talks about him with his therapist, and I hope that's enough.'

Ronen sent the alimony he owed, she told Gil when he asked. Or rather, his family did. His parents deposited money in her account every month and they also came to visit Eran once or twice a month, when they were in the area. She wanted to tell them not to come because she thought their visits only caused Eran pain, but his therapist asked him if he enjoyed the visits with Grandma and Grandpa and he said yes.

WAS IT BECAUSE OF what she told him that night that Gil was so patient with her? Then again, he'd always acted as if he had all the time in the world. He didn't pressure her to see him and always let her initiate their dates. He always offered to pay but did not insist when she objected, and she demanded that they split the bill every time they ate something, allowing him to pay only if they'd just had drinks and the bill was small. He had money, that was implied by things he'd said on their first date, but he didn't flaunt it. After one of their dates she spotted him getting into his car, a new-looking red Kia Sportage. And he did manage to surprise her sometimes, to make her feel there were things she didn't know, that beneath his unremarkable exterior was a more interesting person. When they talked on the phone once, she asked, 'How was your week?' and Gil said, 'I got back from three days in Warsaw yesterday,' even though he hadn't told her anything about taking a trip.

'Warsaw? Holiday or work?'

'Work. Why would anyone go to Warsaw on holiday?'

In the Japanese restaurant, after they'd talked about Eran and Ronen, she tried to change the subject and force herself to be more cheerful, to pull herself out of the descent. 'So what do you do on the evenings we don't meet, if you don't mind me asking?'

Gil said he usually read. He got back from the office at around half past six or seven, eight if he went to the gym, and if the girls were at his place he spent time with them. Sometimes they had supper together, sometimes they watched the news or an episode of a TV series they liked. Now it was something awful called *The Walking Dead*, and he didn't connect with zombies, but he watched it for their sake. If the girls weren't there, or after they left, he generally just read. Before the divorce he hadn't read much, but now, even though the two things were unrelated, he'd set himself a rule: after work, when he was at home, the computer was off and the mobile phone was silenced. He read non-fiction, biographies, books about espionage, about the Mossad, about World War II, but also popular-science books, like Yuval Noah Harari's *Sapiens*, which Orna had also read. He never watched TV alone, not for ideological reasons but because he'd decided it was a waste of time and that books were much better for clearing his mind after work. Orna was ashamed that she'd assumed he was the more superficial one, even though she hadn't opened a book for over a year, except the ones she read to Eran.

He'd replaced the sweet-chocolatey cologne with something sharper, which she disliked, but they were not at the stage where she could say anything about it. Once during one of their dates, and another time later that night, she briefly thought about him without his clothes on and pictured him standing before her naked. His torso was probably fairer and fuller than Ronen's, not hairy, and his legs less thin and muscular, but maybe slightly longer. She hoped his chest was brawny and not soft. In her imagination, she was almost naked, wearing only her panties, but even in her fantasy they did not touch, only examined each other from a short distance, in a room that was not her bedroom or any other room she recognized. But there was the possibility of touching in the way they stood together, a sense that one body touching another was *possible*.

THE MOST SURPRISING THING that occurred between them in May was the phone calls.

It started in the middle of the month, a few days after their fourth date, which was at an expensive fish restaurant at Tel Aviv Port. As on previous occasions, they didn't plan what would happen afterwards, did not agree to meet again, and one evening, after reading to Eran and cleaning up the kitchen and sitting blankly at the computer, she turned on the TV, watched a few dreadful minutes of *Big Brother* and thought about Gil in his flat, maybe reading. She turned off the TV and sent him a text message, but he didn't reply, and she remembered he'd told her he tried to keep his phone off in the evenings. Then, for some reason, she called him, not from her mobile but from the landline.

Gil answered immediately, even though he couldn't have recognized the number. He hadn't turned off his phone because his younger daughter, Hadass, was still at his place, but he hadn't seen Orna's message.

'So should I call later?' she asked, and he said, 'No, hang on a second. I'm going to the other room.'

The phone conversations were short. And they had no clear purpose. They happened once every three or four days, mostly if they weren't getting together, and always on her initiative. Gil said he wouldn't turn his phone off any more in the evenings, he would just put it on silent, and every time she called he answered. She noticed that she always used her landline, as if reconstructing an experience she remembered from her youth: she was fourteen and had her first boyfriend, Sharon Lugasi from the other class, but she didn't have a phone in her room yet. In order to talk to him privately, she would take the phone from the living room, plug it into the socket in her room and lock herself in. Usually his mother answered and she would ask a question no one asks any more: 'Hello, is Sharon at home?'

In those days, too, not unlike in her conversations with Gil, she was unsure why they were talking on the phone at all. They spent all day at school together and didn't have much to say, yet still those phone calls were essential to what was going on between them, even if they consisted mostly of silence.

With Gil there were no silences.

'So how was work? Did you pop over to Moscow and back?'

'Not today. I was in the office all day.'

'No gym? I hope for your sake you skipped lunch at least.'

'No, I didn't make it to the gym. The girls let me know they were both coming and they wanted supper. Maybe first thing tomorrow. I really need to.'

'Are you reading?'

'Not yet. How are you? How's Eran?'

Hearing him say Eran's name flooded her with ambivalence, even aversion. It bothered her that she wasn't telling Eran any more details about Gil and their dates, and kept saying she was going out with a friend. Her mother had already asked if she was seeing someone, but she'd refused to answer.

She hadn't told him that these talks reminded her of those phone calls with Sharon Lugasi. She didn't want him to misinterpret her.

After ten or fifteen minutes she took advantage of a lull and said, 'Well, goodnight,' and he said, 'Goodnight.'

4

ERAN'S BIRTHDAY WAS AT the beginning of June.

Orna took a risk: instead of inviting the class to the usual Friday-afternoon party at a local park or at home, which would give parents two child-free hours without much hassle, she had planned a kite-flying party on the beach in Rishon Le'Zion, so that parents would have to drive their kids there and back during siesta time. One parent suggested she rent a minibus, but Orna didn't want that responsibility, and the expenses had already ballooned into much more than she could afford. She did set up a WhatsApp group to help coordinate pickups, and promised the parents cold beer and watermelon if they wanted to stay at the beach instead of driving back and forth.

The party was at half past four, and Orna was there at three, with Eran and her mother and the lovely school counsellor, who had supported Eran since the divorce and was trying to help him integrate socially; she brought her boyfriend to help set up. Orna had invited

Ronen's parents, even though she didn't have to, but they said no. She assumed they were worried about feeling uncomfortable and didn't want to see her mother. They promised to have a separate family party for Eran at their house.

They set out folding tables and put out the food and drinks. At half past three the big straw mats and beanbags she'd rented were delivered, and at four the party entertainer arrived with a crew of three secondary-schoolers. Eran was busy with the drone that Orna's mother had not been able to resist giving him, even though his actual birthday was only the next day. When the batteries ran out, he helped arrange the snacks. The only thing they couldn't plan was the wind.

At twenty to five there were only three kids, and Orna's mother shot her worried glances, but at ten to five most of the other children arrived, in four cars, and the party started. Twenty-eight out of a class of thirty-three had turned up, and two had told her in advance they wouldn't make it. She didn't have time to think about it during the party, but that evening, when they opened the presents at home, she felt overwhelmed with gratitude to the parents, the children, the entertainer, even her mother, and everyone who had helped her make this the best birthday Eran had ever had. It was proof not only of her organizational skills but of how much the kids and parents loved Eran and saw him as an integral part of the class despite him being so introverted and reclusive. It also indicated their willingness to help him through the crisis. She did not discuss the divorce with most of the parents, but they all clearly knew what she and Eran were going through.

The entertainer divided the kids and those parents who wanted to participate into four groups, and they assembled and decorated the kites. They finished at about quarter to six, and since the wind was too low, they ate the food and lit the candles on the cake. Orna had made lists, but she'd forgotten to bring a chair to hoist Eran up on. One of the dads suggested a beanbag, and that was even better because Eran lay in it with his head lolling back and his eyes on the sky while they swung him up in the air ten times. When the sun started to set, the wind picked up and the kites flew like giant butterflies, drawing curious onlookers; who gathered around them on the beach. Even Orna's mother had to admit that it had been a good idea and that Orna's insistence on a beach party had been justified, and when she handed a cheque to the entertainer at the end of the party, she did so without haggling or giving everyone the impression that she was being exploited, the way she usually did. All in all, they spent almost two thousand five hundred shekels on the party.

ON SATURDAY THEY HAD a quiet day at home.

Eran woke up early and came into her bed to wake her, and she sang 'Happy Birthday', whispering into his ear. She gave him the simple gift she'd bought, after much deliberation and consultation with the therapist: a notebook with thick, blank pages, in a leather binding that fastened with a string, where he could write the date at the top of each page, followed by what he'd done and seen and thought that day. He ran to his room and came back to her in the kitchen after a few minutes to show her what he'd written. She hadn't explained that you were supposed to start on the first page, and he'd filled a page in the middle of the book with large green felt-tipped letters: 'It's my 9 birthday. Mum boat me a notebook. Maybe dad will fone on the computer.' For lunch she made his favourite dish – chicken liver with fried onions and mashed potatoes – and they ate together with her mother, who brought another chocolate cake, this one without candles.

'Didn't he call to say happy birthday?' Orna's mother asked, and Orna didn't answer, just kept clearing the dishes and loading the dishwasher. She was amazed to hear her mother murmur from the dining table, 'That bastard.' Eran was watching TV in his room.

She'd consulted Eran's therapist about how to broach the topic of his dad not being there for his birthday, and the therapist had said he thought Ronen should be compelled to at least phone. So she'd swallowed her pride and sent him an email and a Skype message, for the first time in months: 'I hope you remember that it's Eran's birthday on Saturday. It would really help if you called to say happy birthday.' Ronen didn't write back, but she hoped he'd seen the messages.

Her mother left in the afternoon, and then it was just the two of them. She suggested they go to a movie, but Eran said he'd rather stay home, and she realized he was waiting for Ronen to call. They played Monopoly in the living room and then Eran shut himself in his room again and watched TV, and she marked exams. Skype was on and active every time she glanced at it. And there was nothing wrong with the internet. She felt her hatred mounting and tried to control it, because it wouldn't help Eran and in fact would only hurt him. She mustn't let Ronen ruin the fact that she had given Eran two blissful days, that she'd managed to do it even under these circumstances, alone, or rather with the help of people who loved them.

In the evening, before reading a story, she said more or less what she'd agreed with the therapist she'd say in case Ronen didn't get in touch: 'Dad hasn't been able to call yet, but I'm sure he'll talk to you soon, and I know he's thinking about you and about how you're already nine. You know there's a big time difference between us and where Dad is, right? It might be because of that. Anyway, you know Dad loves you very, very, very much, right?'

She wanted to call Ronen and curse him the way her mother had, but it was pointless. He wouldn't answer. Instead she tried Gil, but his phone was off. The last time they'd talked, on Tuesday evening, she'd told him about the party preparations, and before hanging up she'd said, 'We'll probably only talk afterwards.' On Friday he'd texted her first thing in the morning: 'Good luck today! And happy birthday to both of you.'

She had to talk to someone, so she called Sophie, and within a minute she was bawling, offloading all the week's tension. Sophie's husband, Itzik, was home and Sophie said she could come over, even though it was late. She lived five minutes away, and at quarter to ten she was there, wearing a tracksuit. They talked about Ronen, and Sophie told Orna exactly what she wanted to hear – whispering, so Eran wouldn't wake up: that it was hard to believe what a shit he was, that no one could have imagined he'd turn into such a louse and that he didn't deserve an amazing son like Eran.

That was comforting.

And that was when, without meaning to, Orna told her about Gil.

Sophie had said, 'God will compensate you for that shit, I'm sure someone good will come along eventually,' and Orna amazed her by saying, 'I may already be going out with someone, I'm not sure. But I think I am.'

Sophie couldn't believe Orna hadn't mentioned it yet, and she wanted to know everything. Orna told her some things that were not easy to tell. That they'd met on a site for divorced singles and had gone out seven or eight times. That they talked on the phone every so often. Sophie wanted to see what he looked like, and since Orna didn't have a picture on her phone, Sophie said, 'No problem, we'll find him on Facebook.' It was strange that Orna had never thought to do that, but then again she wasn't on Facebook herself. They logged on to Sophie's account, searched for 'Gil Hamtzani', in Hebrew and in English, in various spellings, but couldn't find him. Then Orna remembered they could see his pictures on the dating site and she clicked on his profile. Sophie remarked, 'Not bad-looking, but he's a bit old, isn't he?'

They flipped through a few more profiles, just out of curiosity. 'These guys are pretty cute,' Sophie decreed. 'Maybe I should get divorced too.' Then she asked, 'So, is it serious?'

Orna replied, 'I have no idea. How do you even know? I think I've forgotten.'

Her mood was improved. Gil was no longer a secret, and she felt that this somehow brought them closer. She admitted that they hadn't had sex or even kissed, and Sophie exclaimed, 'Well then, how exactly are you expecting to know? Sleep with him, then we'll talk!' Orna laughed. It was like a conversation between secondary-school girls, even though they hadn't known each other in high school and had only become friends much later, through the boys. Eran and Tom, Sophie's eldest, had been in the same nursery school and then kindergarten, but Tom was on the spectrum and they'd sent him to a special-needs school.

AND THE NEXT DAY it happened.

Gil wasn't available all Sunday, which was unusual for him, and he only called her back at six. He asked how the party had been, and she told him it was a big success. When she mentioned that she'd been trying to get hold of him since the day before, he surprised her again. It turned out that he'd made a spontaneous decision – partly because he knew she'd be busy with Eran's birthday and they wouldn't be able to meet – to go on a bike-riding trip in Cyprus for a long weekend with friends from his cycling group. A spot had opened up when someone had cancelled at the last minute and he'd decided to go for it and did not regret the decision. They'd cycled a beautiful route, from the peak of the Troodos Mountains all the way to the coastal town of Paphos, through pine forests and ancient villages. They'd had great food and stayed in a lovely hotel in Paphos. He said all his muscles ached, and she assumed he wouldn't want to meet, but when she asked he said he just needed to check with the girls, because they might be coming for dinner, and he'd get back to her soon. At half past six he texted: 'I rescheduled with the girls for tomorrow. Want to meet at nine?'

And she knew this would be a different date even before they met.

Not because of him, because he would probably have kept going the same way as before, but because she felt different. Everything blended and came together: the fact that Gil was no longer a secret because she'd talked about him out loud with Sophie; Eran's birthday, which had gone off without a hitch; the fact that Ronen hadn't called or answered her messages; the way Sophie had been matter-of-fact about her dating someone and at times had even seemed jealous.

Gil's face was suntanned from riding, and he looked younger, in a red T-shirt. She really did feel happy to see him. They went to an Asian restaurant in the food market at Tel Aviv Port. They sat at the bar, so their knees touched every so often – his in blue jeans, hers bare, because the dress she wore hiked up when she sat down.

She felt free of secrets and prohibitions and guilt. She amplified her sense of freedom by trying to speak openly and directly, and every so often she put her hand on his knee. After telling Gil in great detail about the party, because he asked her to, and after he had shown her pictures on his phone of the views they'd seen on the ride – from a website, because he hadn't taken any pictures himself – she said to him, without knowing she was going to say it, 'Can I ask you a hypothetical question?' Gil said hypothetical questions were lawyers' favourite kind.

'What does one do in this situation usually, when you want to be together... you know, intimately?'

It took him a minute to understand. 'Do you mean, where do we go? Which home?'

She said, 'Mmmhm,' and he looked surprised. It was as if they'd never met as man and woman before, and now it was a real date.

'You usually go to one person's flat.'

But she didn't want to go to his place. Both because she felt it was too early and because she was afraid one of his daughters would show up unannounced. Her place wasn't an option, even though she'd considered it briefly when she'd asked her mother to have Eran sleep over and take him to school the next morning.

'So where do you go? A car? The beach? Hypothetically, of course.'

Gil stammered, said it depended, and when she asked where he'd gone with other women he'd dated, he said a hotel was an option.

She was reluctant at first. How had she not thought of that? 'A hotel with hourly rates? Like in the movies? Isn't that a bit sleazy?'

'I don't know what kind of movies you mean, but it doesn't have to be an hourly hotel. It could be any hotel in Tel Aviv. You get a room for the night.'

After the initial aversion, she actually liked the idea, though she wasn't sure why. 'So what do you think? Isn't it time for us?' she said.

'I hope so. But are you sure about tonight? My muscles are still a bit stiff from cycling... And isn't it late for you?' She wanted to be home by one or two at the latest, so she could get in a few hours' sleep before teaching, but it was only ten. She asked if he knew any hotels, and she could tell the question embarrassed him. He said, 'There are signs all over town, and we could also look online.' She searched on her phone.

HE DROVE THERE IN his Kia Sportage and she in her old Suzuki. She could still have changed her mind on the way, but she didn't. On the contrary, she was anxious to get into the hotel room, to be with him in bed, to sleep with him so she would know what it was like, to sleep with him so that it would be behind her.

And the hotel surprised her.

It was small, located on an ordinary residential street, but it looked like a hotel. With a narrow, cosy lobby and clean carpeting, two bookshelves and a coffee-and-tea station, and a couple of Chinese or Japanese tourists waiting for a taxi on a brown leather couch.

She was the one who'd initiated, who'd pressed, who'd been daring, not because she'd decided to be but because she'd been possessed of a vague knowledge that this was the only way it would happen, the only way she would feel she wanted it.

She turned to him as soon as the door shut behind him and kissed him, pressed up against him, and lifted her dress above her waist to feel him rubbing against her. Then she pulled him to the bed and took off his shirt and touched his soft back, and when he took off his trousers before she could, she began to feel herself leaving the room for a moment. But she quickly brought herself back in by putting her hand on his and saying, 'Not yet, wait a second.'

The room was an ordinary hotel room, where any tourist looking for something not too fancy could sleep: parquet floor, white sheets, black-and-white photograph of Tel Aviv in the fifties, medium-sized Toshiba television on the wall. A dark curtain hid a window that she later discovered looked out on the peeling, shabby wall of a dilapidated block of flats that was too close, with pipes and cables and old air-conditioning units.

She thought it would take her time to get used to his skin, which was too light and soft, and to the many birthmarks on his back and shoulders, but she knew she could become familiar with this body.

Gil was gentle, sometimes too gentle, touching her hair more than she would have liked, and he didn't kiss her neck and stomach enough, but all in all the sex wasn't bad, for a first time. He came inside her, wearing a condom, and she didn't come, and when he asked if she wanted him to go on with his finger she said, 'Not right now. Maybe later.' His eyes were open all the time, searching for hers, and she thought about how she'd never been with a man who didn't shut his eyes during sex even once.

GIL WENT TO THE bathroom right afterwards to shower, locking the door, and Orna turned on the reading lamp and looked at her phone to see if there were any messages from her mum – and then for an instant she saw her body. Her feet, her toenails painted black, her pubic hair, which she hadn't shaved for a long while, her thick, dark nipples.

She did think about Ronen, too, but her main thought was something else:

Eran is asleep in the room where I grew up, in my mother's house, and Ronen is in Nepal with a German woman named Ruth. And I am here, in a hotel room in Tel Aviv, after having sex with a man. With Gil. Maybe it'll happen again and maybe not. We fell apart but I am whole.

There was another thought too: Ronen remembered her body from when she was twenty-five, and thirty, the body before the pregnancy and the body after childbirth, and when she slept with him she was an amalgamation of all those bodies, as if the memory of them were with them in bed. For Gil, though, this body she had now – this stomach, these feet, these breasts – was the only body she had, the way it was today, the way she was today. She didn't know if that was good or bad.

Gil didn't say much, as though he were a bit stunned. He came out of the shower after a long time, and when she went in there was hardly any shampoo or shower gel left in the bright little bottles. He walked her to her car, but they didn't kiss. Orna asked, 'Are you sure you're okay?' and he said he was. His back and leg muscles hurt. He said he hadn't thought this was going to happen today, and she said she hadn't either. There was a new sort of intimacy, even in the way they walked next to each other on the narrow, dark Tel Aviv street to the car. Then Gil said, 'It feels strange for you to go back to your place now, and me to mine. It's almost 2 a.m. Are you sure you don't want to come over?'

She didn't.

And she said, 'So we'll talk tomorrow?'

5

THEY DID TALK THE next day. And in fact almost every day for the next couple of weeks. They met at least once a week, mostly at the hotel and once in his flat. It was as if they were trying to intensify things, to test themselves and their relationship, turning up the heat to know if they should let the dish keep cooking. Yet despite the frequent meetings, she still wasn't sure, and she vacillated between thinking it should go on and feeling like a stranger with Gil.

She liked the hotel. Sunshine Beach Hotel. The hours they spent there were like the short trips overseas that Orna had grown accustomed to when she'd worked as a flight attendant, which she'd been missing dearly in the past few years. White sheets that someone else laundered and smoothed over the large bed. Heavy curtains that concealed the same view from every room. Her mother stayed with Eran overnight once, and Orna and Gil slept in the hotel and ate breakfast next to a pair of older tourists, sunburnt Germans who tried to strike up a conversation with them. Orna didn't know what to tell them, and wondered if they realized what she and Gil were doing there or if they assumed they were husband and wife, but Gil chatted comfortably in English, advising them to take a taxi to the Dead Sea rather than a bus or a hired car. When they asked where he and his wife were from, he said they were Israeli but had been living in Europe for a few years and were here for a visit. Then he smiled at her the way Eran sometimes did when he managed to 'pull one over on Grandma'.

He suggested they meet in his flat, and Orna continued to refuse until one evening, after a movie, they went to the hotel and there were no rooms available. It was in the early summer and Tel Aviv was already full of tourists. Gil promised there was no chance the girls would be at his place or turn up unannounced. He'd already told her that he'd asked them to call from now on before they came, and he'd even offered to take the keys back from them if it would reassure her. She agreed to go, but she felt uncomfortable in the flat. It was clean, probably because he had a cleaner, but it hadn't been renovated for a long time and was full of dated furniture. It felt like being in someone's recently deceased parents' flat: old wooden sideboard in the living room, glass-doored cabinet with porcelain figurines, well-worn sofa facing a huge flat-screen television. She'd never been in a divorcé's home before, but she had somehow imagined it differently, partly because he'd told her that he'd put quite a bit of money into it. The girls' rooms were almost empty. Light-coloured kids' beds with matching desks, and that was it. In one of them she spotted a football. The bed in Gil's room was old, and there was a dressing table. The bedroom window looked out on to a pretty inner courtyard with lots of trees.

And nothing became any clearer. The second time they slept together Gil was more confident and his erection was stronger and lasted longer, and she wondered if he'd taken Viagra, even though she'd never had sex with a man on Viagra before. He still touched her hair more than she would have liked, and she had not grown accustomed to his body even after the fifth or sixth time – although she did manage to come with him from the third time. There was something spongy about his body, not fat but too soft, not muscular. After he came he hurried to the bathroom to wipe himself off and shower, and she couldn't help remembering Ronen, who used to get philosophical after they slept together, as if sex put him deeper into himself and into the world. He could lie on the bed for hours afterwards, talking, without moving or getting dressed or wiping off the semen or sweat. He was shorter than Gil but thin and very dark – he had the body of an anorexic dancer, as she told him after one of their first times – and his hair had hardly changed since the day they'd met. Black, long, tied in a ponytail at the back of his neck. Three years ago the first silver hairs had started to appear.

JUNE COMES TO AN end. Summer holidays. Eran had asked to go to camp at school with all his schoolfriends, and she'd agreed. The birthday party had improved his social standing, and he even had a classmate named Roi over one afternoon.

Her mornings, after she walks Eran to camp, become slow and long. She marks matriculation exams, turns on the air conditioning and turns it back off when it gets too cold, and at twelve makes herself something for lunch. When she's near the supermarket she picks up a free newspaper and goes over the classifieds, curious about part-time jobs or a higher-paying teaching job, even though she has no real desire to leave her job, nor any plans to apply for head of year or head teacher. She sees ads for lawyers offering foreign passport application services, but none of them is for Gil Hamtzani.

He goes abroad a lot, and they see less of each other. Three days in Bucharest in the first week of July, four days in Bulgaria in the second week. Their dates and phone calls become less frequent, though it's not clear who is driving that. Perhaps it's both of them, but it's not as if they make a decision and let each other know that things aren't working out.

Everyone around her is going away or planning to. Sophie and Itzik take a three-week trip to the east coast of the US. The downstairs neighbours ask Orna to water their plants while they're on holiday in Thailand. Eran's therapist is also planning a long summer trip, and she meets him before he leaves. He sums up the past year for Eran, at school and at home, and says there is still a long way to go but he thinks Eran is coping well. Eran understands that Dad didn't leave because of him and his difficulties, but because he chose a new wife and a new job, a new country and a new life, and he still loves Eran even from afar. It's been more than a month since Eran's birthday, and Ronen still hasn't answered her messages, but Eran hasn't mentioned him. Eran writes fairly regularly in the notebook she bought him and brings it to his therapy sessions, voluntarily. He manages to write about his fears in a way that is surprisingly direct for his age, but also writes about a lot of happy moments at school and at camp with his friends. He is still slightly detached from the other kids, he keeps them at arm's length, but he is an observant and insightful boy, and his rare ability to verbally describe what he sees and feels is developing. Towards the end of their meeting, the therapist asks Orna about the man she's dating, both because she'd mentioned him and because, as it turns out, Eran has told him about the 'friend' Mum sees sometimes. Orna is embarrassed. She apologizes for not updating him, as if she had an obligation to do so, and admits that she once stayed out all night and left Eran with her mother. To her surprise, the therapist says he sees this as a positive. He encourages her to tell Eran more, to say that she's going out for fun or going on a trip with the friend, so that Eran can see that she is also starting a new life. If she tells him everything, or almost everything, Eran will probably be less afraid that in her new life, as in his father's, he will have no place. When the therapist asks if she is planning to have them meet, she immediately says, 'Who? Eran and Gil? No chance,' and realizes that at least for now she feels she will not be able to do that, even if their relationship continues.

*

ORNA'S MOTHER INTERROGATES HER about Gil and, having asked her to stay with Eran overnight, Orna can no longer avoid her questions. She tells her his name, says he's a lawyer, gives general details about his office and where he lives and his daughters and his ex-wife, but when her mother wants to know more, she becomes defensive, as she always does, because she thinks her mother is mostly trying to find out if he has any money.

She tells her that when she was gone that night she slept in his flat, and that they go out to movies and restaurants. He's on good terms with his ex-wife but there's no chance of them reconciling.

'How do you know? Aren't they in touch?'

Something about her mother's questions forces her to try to understand why she still isn't sure if the relationship is right or not, and whether Gil really is less excited to see her recently or if she's just imagining it. Sophie suggests that she make a list of pros and cons, which seems unnecessary, so she doesn't write it out, but she can't stop conducting the balance sheet in her mind. Before their dates she is usually happy to be seeing him. They have things to talk about, and she thinks she enjoys their hotel time. But there are also moments when, probably because of what it lacks, the relationship floods her with despair and pain and even self-hatred. She isn't sufficiently attracted to him and isn't sure whether that would change if he lost weight. There are things he does that strike her as compulsive, like the long showers right after sex and the fact that he takes his phone into the bathroom with him, and the way he always places his wallet on top of his phone on the bedside table in the hotel or on the table in restaurants and cafés.

And she doesn't ever want to be in his flat again, although she can't explain why to herself.

She's never visited his office, doesn't know exactly what he does at his job, nor is she curious about it. She didn't see his bike when she was at his place, either inside or down in the lobby. And on one of their last dates he did say something that put her off. They were discussing the political situation; everyone was talking about how there'd been a war last summer and since things were heating up again along the southern border and there'd been rockets fired into Israel, they wondered if there'd be another war this summer. Gil remarked that these little wars were good for his business. 'My accountant was the one who first noticed it, because you can see it on the income graph,' he explained. 'After every military operation, anyone who is eligible and hasn't done it yet rushes out to get a foreign passport, to sort of have a Plan B in case we don't survive the next war, or just because it's more pleasant to get into foreign countries with a European passport.'

SHE ASSUMED THE AFFAIR would fade away of its own accord. That, in fact, it already was.

She sensed that Gil wouldn't fight for the relationship and knew she herself wouldn't insist on it, and perhaps that was a sign that it was best to let go. Eran's camp would be over in mid-August, and she'd have to find a way to pass the two weeks before school started, so she'd be exhausted in the evenings anyway. Then it would be autumn and she'd have something left over from her relationship with Gil, even if it was finished: when she used the dating site again, which she probably would, she'd be more experienced. Perhaps she'd know how to read the profiles and look at the pictures differently, and when she met someone it would be something beyond just new and frightening.

But suddenly he started phoning more. He said he'd had a couple of busy weeks at work and asked if she was planning any trips. She said she wasn't. She'd be happy to take Eran to Amsterdam or London for a week, or to a quiet Greek island, but it was too expensive right now, and her mother, who in the spring had seemed likely to offer to help them go on holiday and maybe even join them, had informed Orna that she was going on a package tour of Croatia and Slovenia on the High Holy Days and didn't mention the possibility of helping out again. Gil asked if there was a chance that she'd go away with him for a few days at the end of August, his treat, and she said no. She couldn't leave Eran for a week – even one night had been difficult for her, and also she wasn't clear on the status of their relationship and it seemed too soon for them to go on holiday together.

Gil asked, 'What do you mean? What aren't you clear on?'

'I don't know. Are things clear to you?'

'What's clear to me is that I enjoy being with you.'

What had she expected him to say? She couldn't even say that much to him without reservations. And she secretly thanked him for being subtle enough not to ask her the obvious: don't you enjoy being with me?

A few minutes after that call he texted her:

Then how about a weekend away in Israel? A B&B in the Golan? You need a holiday too, don't you? We can go this weekend if it works for you, I'd be really into it.

She debated and wrote several messages and deleted them before replying:

This weekend doesn't work.

A WEEK LATER THEY went to Jerusalem.

Gil came to pick her up on Friday morning, and Eran and her mother watched from the window behind semi-shut blinds as she got into his car, Orna having told her mother there was no chance she'd ask Gil to come up. She didn't take a suitcase but a medium-sized handbag with toiletries and make-up, a phone charger, a change of clothes and a book she'd started reading on mornings with Eran on the beach. Before packing she'd laid out what she was taking on her bed, the way she used to do before trips. His Kia Sportage was high and spacious and amazingly clean, inside and out, and it was freezing cold from the air conditioning. Gil leaned over and kissed her on the lips after she put her bag on the back seat. The radio was tuned to the classical music station, and when the car pulled away in a strange silence, as though floating above the road, the realisation spread through her that she was really going on holiday. For the first time in who knows how long.

Gil had booked a room at the Scottish Guesthouse, in a church above the Valley of Hinnom, for the night of the twenty-first of August.

Orna had wanted to stay there for years, and immediately fell in love with the modest, practical rooms and everything around them: the shaded gravel courtyard behind the church, with coffee tables and chairs scattered around haphazardly, and the two tables set out near the entrance with a view of East Jerusalem. They drank coffee there after settling into their room, which was ready even though they were early. It wasn't a luxury hotel, but it was peaceful and had a simple beauty, which she felt was exactly what she needed.

The midday temperature climbed up to 36 degrees, but they still spent the day outside. They strolled around the historic neighbourhoods of Yemin Moshe and Mishkenot Sha'ananim, then crossed the main road and walked into the eastern part of the city. At lunchtime they took a cab downtown, to the Machane Yehuda market. They had a small lunch of hot cheese bourekas at a market stall, because Gil had booked a restaurant for an early supper. At four they went back to the hotel to rest, and they had sex, and it was better than it had been before, maybe because it was early in the day and the room had a dark, pleasant coolness and there was a sense of freedom. The restaurant was near the hotel, so they walked. They drank a whole bottle of wine and talked with greater frankness than before, more thanks to him than to her.

He asked about Eran and Ronen, and she told him Ronen had finally called last Saturday, and had told Eran he was planning to visit soon, maybe on Sukkot. She wasn't sure if it would really happen and she also wasn't sure if it would make her happy – in fact she knew it scared her very much, but she could see that the possibility of his father visiting was thrilling for Eran. She was fearful ahead of the start of the new school year, as she always was, because she didn't know who Eran's teacher was going to be and if they would understand him and be patient with him. But the way last year had ended and Eran's decision to go to the school camp had given her hope that he was opening up and starting to make friends.

Gil was relaxed, even more than on their usual dates in Tel Aviv, possibly because he hadn't been at work all day, and she thought about how he almost never got a call on his mobile when they were together. On the way to the hotel there was a nice breeze, almost cool, and Gil said, 'We've known each other for almost four months now, haven't we?'

'Almost? It's more than four, I think.'

'And you still won't tell me what you think.'

'About what?'

'About us. About me. About what's going on between us.'

She walked quietly, thinking, and then said, 'It's a bit hard to put these things into words, isn't it?'

He just wanted her to know that he understood why it was difficult for her, how complicated it was, and that he wasn't in a hurry. It felt good for her to hear that, but when he added that as far as he was concerned, if she wanted to, they could continue more or less the way things were, she felt that something about his words was jarring – it almost sounded like a job offer.

That night they had sex again, and it was shorter. He hurried to the shower afterwards, for the second time that day, and then he went to his car because he'd left something in the boot, and he came back after more than twenty minutes, by which time she was almost asleep.

In the morning she awoke to the sound of water running in the shower and realized he'd got up before her. He'd left his phone next to the bed this time, underneath his wallet, either because he'd forgotten to take it into the bathroom or because he thought she was asleep. Orna picked it up, and when she found it didn't require a password she quickly flipped through the apps. She even opened his WhatsApp for a moment, but she had no time to see anything unusual and she put the phone back when she heard the water being turned off.

Three days later she saw him with his wife.

6

TUESDAY, THE LAST WEEK of the summer holidays. In the morning she had a staff meeting ahead of the new school year, and she took Eran with her; he played on his tablet in the office. Her schedule was almost identical to last year's, even though she had two new Year Ten classes. She'd promised Eran a fun day out in Tel Aviv afterwards, the last one for the summer. They'd do a craft workshop at the Tel Aviv Museum, lunch at McDonald's and see a movie at the Dizengoff Centre mall.

She saw Gil when they reached the third floor on the escalator, as soon as they turned left towards the box office. He was standing in the queue at a juice bar with two young girls who Orna immediately knew were his daughters, Noa and Hadass. For a moment she thought of turning back, or ignoring him and walking past without saying a word – Gil hadn't seen her because he was trying to get the attention of the young girl with piercings behind the counter – but that was stupid, and she thought maybe this was the right way to introduce him to Eran, just by chance, without making a big deal out of it, when he was with his girls. She whispered to Eran, 'See that man standing there with the girls? That's the friend I told you about, who I sometimes meet.' In the seconds that passed between when she noticed him and when they were standing behind him, a woman appeared next to him, or perhaps she'd been there before but Orna hadn't noticed her because she hadn't thought to make the connection.

Orna said, 'Hi, Gil,' and he turned to her. He looked surprised. Not startled. They hadn't talked since the weekend in Jerusalem, because she was busy with preparations for the school year and Gil had said he was going away for three days, she couldn't remember exactly when, but they'd planned to meet this weekend and she'd been looking forward to it after Jerusalem. If he'd tried to kiss her on the lips or the cheek in front of Eran she would have pulled back, but something in his response paralysed her. He was distant, indifferent even, and his expression remained unchanged as he quickly scrutinized Eran. She said, 'This is Eran,' and Gil said, 'Nice to meet you, Eran,' and then turned to his daughters and added, 'This is Orna Azran, an old client of mine.' Her first thought was that he had said that because of the girls, and she might have continued to think so if not for the woman, who was trying to be friendly to both of them, but especially to Eran. 'Nice to meet you,' she said with a smile, 'I'm Ruthi, his wife. Are you also going to the movies?'

*

ERAN WATCHED THE MOVIE transfixed, and Orna thought about Gil as anger and hurt pride surged inside her. In the hours that followed, she was upset, but not all of the time. It came in waves. Gil had been lying to her for over four months. Was he really married? It seemed so. Even though there was a chance that Ruthi was his ex-wife and had introduced herself as his wife because she was used to doing so, or because there was no point introducing yourself to strangers as 'his ex-wife'. Gil had told her they were on good terms and sometimes saw each other. But if that was the case, then why had he introduced Orna as 'an old client'?

She urged Eran to skip the ice cream and promised him he could watch TV at home. On the way she tried not to think about Gil so as not to lose her concentration while she was driving. The afternoon traffic from Tel Aviv to Holon was heavy, and Eran was in a talkative mood, so she turned the radio on. He didn't say anything about Gil and didn't seem to notice what had happened to her after seeing him. When they got home, she turned on the TV in his room and logged on to her computer as if she had something urgent to do, but she didn't know what to do. She went on to the dating site and opened up Gil's profile and stared at it. He hadn't called or texted yet, maybe because he was still on his family outing. At half past seven, an hour before the usual time, they'd already had supper and showered, and she read Eran only two pages of a book, explained that she was tired and asked him to try to fall asleep on his own.

Sophie was still in the States, and Orna would never tell her mother. Her instinct in times of distress was still to talk to Ronen, but that was out of the question, and he wouldn't have answered anyway.

She got into bed, and when she lay down she felt as if she were suffocating. She was as scared as she'd been on those first few nights after Ronen left. She didn't turn on the light in her bedroom or get up and the fear did not fade until she fell asleep. There were so many things she didn't understand: his relaxed air whenever they met, his flat, the way he always answered when she phoned and was almost always free to meet whenever she wanted to, the nights they'd spent together at the hotel and the weekend in Jerusalem. The fact that he'd never behaved secretively. That didn't fit with the possibility of him being married. When she woke up at quarter past five in the morning she had no messages or missed calls from him, and she knew then with certainty that he would not get in touch with her, that he would not call to explain, that he was planning to simply disappear from her life without a word.

ON FRIDAY THE SCHOOL year began. She walked Eran to his school and stayed with him until the first bell rang, and then drove to work. What hadn't left her in those first few days was the fear. She did not feel shame, nor did she feel betrayed – in fact, she thought that Gil didn't owe her anything – there was just a fear that grew stronger and stronger, as though she'd been the victim of an extremely violent act.

In the evenings she checked three times to make sure she'd locked the door and shut the windows, and she called her mother after Eran fell asleep, ostensibly to find out how she was. The only time she allowed herself to talk about it was with Sophie, who phoned a few days after she got back from the States, and that conversation helped her, but in an unexpected way. They met at a café on a Monday morning. She waited patiently while Sophie described the exhausting weekend standing in queue for rides at Disney World and the hotel in Miami and then, when Sophie asked how it was going with the guy Orna was dating, she confessed, 'Not so well. I think he's married.'

Sophie was outraged. She had no doubt that Gil was married and that the woman at the mall was his wife. And she couldn't understand why Orna wasn't doing anything about it. 'What am I supposed to do?' Orna asked, and Sophie said, 'What are you supposed to do? Go to the police, or at least post something on Facebook – what do you mean?!' When Orna asked why she should go to the police, Sophie replied, 'Because it's rape, no less than that. It's obvious. He lied to you so he could ... You know very well why, and it doesn't matter that you consented, because you didn't know who he really was. If he'd told you he was a pilot, or a billionaire, it would have been the same thing.'

But Orna wasn't sure that was how she felt. Or that Sophie understood her and Gil's relationship. More to the point, she felt that this wasn't the issue – and certainly not the reason for her fear. She didn't feel as if she had been raped. He was an asshole who'd lied to her, just like Sophie said, that was clear, but he hadn't tried to force himself on her, and they probably wouldn't have had sex to that day if she hadn't initiated it, they'd just have had dinners and movies. What did he actually want from her? He hadn't pressured her, hadn't courted her; she was the one who'd contacted him through the site, and if she'd disappeared he wouldn't have called her. So what was the whole production for? And the lies – if he had lied to her? And the stories he'd made up, like about his girls staying over at his place and the divorce agreement? She felt that the source of her fear was something different. That perhaps it had something to do with what had happened with Ronen. A delayed fear, repressed all this time, that she would never get over what had happened to her and would never find someone else. That she would be alone. And she thought that Ronen's acts were far worse than Gil's, because he'd also betrayed Eran and lied to him and then abandoned him, and she couldn't go to the police to file a complaint against Gil. Hadn't Ronen been lying when he'd said his overseas trips with tour groups weren't driving them apart but in fact bringing them closer because they made him miss her? Hadn't it taken him weeks, maybe months, to tell her about Ruth? And he, unlike Gil, did have an obligation to tell her the truth, if only because they had a child together.

She told Sophie she wasn't going to file a complaint. Sophie said, 'I can't understand you. Why would you let him get away with this? Besides, there's no way this is the first time he's done it, and it's probably not the last either.' Orna replied, 'Because it's not my personality. Come on, how long have you known me?'

Sophie said, 'Then I wish it was your personality,' and Orna thought she was insinuating that if it had been, Ronen wouldn't have left her either, but that was probably not what Sophie meant.

Instead of going to the police, she sent Gil a text message one evening in early September:

Aren't you planning to apologize? Explain?

She could tell that the message had been read, but Gil didn't answer.

7

THE DAYS WENT BY. It was mid-September. Everyone was back from their summer travels and planning their next trips, for Sukkot in October. Eran's year had started off rockier than the last one, and sometimes he refused to get out of bed in the morning. The transition from Year Four to Year Five was complicated and demanded more concentration and effort in class and at home. The teachers seemed less patient too. Orna met Eran's new teacher, who tried to reassure her, insisting that lots of pupils struggled at the beginning of Year Five and Orna had nothing to worry about because they all had their fingers on the pulse. But Orna felt, perhaps unjustly, that the teacher's words of encouragement concealed a note of criticism at her parenting, and that she might be hinting that Orna should get Eran diagnosed.

Eran's therapist also sensed difficulties. He thought it might be a delayed response to the crisis at home and suggested stepping up to two sessions a week, but she couldn't ask her mother to pay for that. He didn't ask about Gil, nor did she mention him. Her mother did ask about the lawyer she was dating, and Orna dismissed her: 'Nothing came of it in the end.'

Gil's profile was still on the dating site, unchanged. 'Forty-two years old, divorced once.'

She didn't log on often, because she felt it was all behind her and she knew she wouldn't make contact again with anyone there. She deleted her own profile.

Sophie suggested she open a Facebook account, since there were networks of friends, which made everything more transparent, and it was much harder to lie. But Orna resisted: lots of teachers said Facebook opened an unwanted door for students and parents, and also, she didn't want her romantic efforts to be conducted in public. When she did go on the dating site and look at Gil's profile, it was almost out of pure curiosity, to see if he'd changed anything. Once she even thought of creating a new account for herself, with a false name and a fake picture, which she would use to get in touch with him and see how he responded – would he try to get the conversation going the same way, and repeat the same stories he'd told her almost six months ago? But she assumed he would recognize her writing style, and there really wasn't any point, either in that or in going to his flat (she thought she could find it even though she didn't remember the address) to conduct stakeouts, as she had once considered doing.

She remembered that the one and only time she'd been at his place, she'd sensed that something was wrong, even if she couldn't say exactly what. What had she really felt that time? That it wasn't his? Perhaps that no one lived there? There was no name on the door, only the flat number, and no food in the refrigerator. Gil had apologized and said he almost always ate out, even though he'd previously told her his girls sometimes came over for supper. The soap by the bathroom sink was dark and dried out, as if it hadn't been used for weeks, but Gil was a man who washed his hands frequently. There were other things she'd noticed: no sign of the bike he'd told her about, either in the flat or downstairs, for example.

When she thought back to that evening in his flat, for the first time in several days, Orna felt furious again, but this time it was accompanied not by fear but by detective-like curiosity. She texted Gil:

> I've been told to file a police complaint or tell your wife what you do when you're out, or write the truth about you on the dating site, but I haven't done it yet. Are you sure you don't want to explain?

SHE WAS SURPRISED TO find herself capable of such a firm and implicitly threatening tone.

She saw that the message had reached him, and he answered after a few minutes:

> I'm glad you didn't. Thanks. Can I call?

FOR AN INSTANT THE fear returned. She didn't want to hear his voice or for him to hear hers. It was almost 11 p.m. and the next day she had to start teaching early, and she regretted texting him. She said she preferred that he not call, and he said he wanted to explain but since she'd removed her profile from the site he couldn't write to her over chat. She concluded from this that he'd searched for her on the site, and that he wasn't completely indifferent to what had happened to her since they'd broken up.

'Then explain here,' she wrote, and he answered, 'Okay,' and then added, 'but it'll take a while.'

She cleaned up the kitchen and the living room, and when she went in to shower she put her phone on the bathroom sink, under a towel to protect it from the heat and the steam. When she got into bed with the same book she'd taken on their weekend in Jerusalem, three long messages came in from Gil, probably because what he said couldn't fit in one.

He said he was sorry, he felt terrible about what had happened – 'eating myself up', that was the phrase he used – and he knew Orna couldn't forgive him for what he'd done so he hadn't even tried to explain himself after their chance meeting at Dizengoff Centre.

He and his wife weren't actually divorced but separated, but when he'd met Orna on the dating site they'd both been clear that they could see other people, and that they were headed for divorce. He hadn't put that in his profile or told Orna all the facts because he knew women were reluctant to date men who who hadn't finalized their divorce yet.

A few weeks after they met and started going out, his father's health had deteriorated and shortly afterwards he'd died, plunging Gil into a crisis, and he'd moved back in with his wife and the girls and agreed to give the marriage another chance, even though he knew it wasn't what he wanted. Perhaps he'd also done so because he sensed that Orna wasn't sure about their relationship and thought she was going to break it off. Of course he should have told her everything honestly, but he was ashamed and afraid, and it was hard for him to give her up. He understood that he'd hurt her and he apologized again, and would understand if she told his wife or spread the story some other way. Perhaps he even hoped that's what she'd do, because then he'd have to stop living a lie and be done with this marriage once and for all.

In the end he said he missed her, he hoped one day she would meet a man who deserved her and he envied the person she would allow into her life wholeheartedly. He knew it wasn't him, not only because of what he'd done but also because from the day they'd met he'd felt he was not a man she would choose to live with, even if he really had been divorced.

Orna read his messages twice that night, in bed. And once in the morning before Eran woke up. She felt she couldn't believe a word he said, because there were so many things about his behaviour that the messages didn't explain. Still, his words managed to close up at least part of the open wound, and mostly she felt that her response to the whole story had been correct.

She started to write back to him in the morning, while she

sipped her coffee, but nothing she wrote was accurate, so she didn't send the message that day or in the following days. When she finally did, it was from a different place, and after many things had changed.

8

RONEN GOT IN TOUCH via Skype a week before Rosh Hashanah. It was just after seven, and she and Eran were eating supper. When she saw who was calling, she called Eran to the computer and told him to answer the call himself.

They only talked for a few minutes, and while they did Orna waited anxiously in the kitchen. She could barely hear Eran's voice because he always spoke quietly with Ronen. He came back to the kitchen and said Dad wanted to talk to her. It was hard for her to look at him on the screen. Ronen said, 'Hi, Orna,' and smiled in a way that made her feel he'd been rehearsing the conversation. He asked if she would be available to talk privately after Eran went to bed. She said yes, and he thanked her. 'So I'll call you in a couple of hours, is that okay?'

When she went back to the dinner table Eran announced: 'Dad's coming to visit on Sukkot. Did he tell you?'

Ronen called back at ten, and she could tell by his punctuality that he wanted to tell her something she didn't want to hear. At first she couldn't figure out if the room she was seeing on the screen was an office or a home. There was a completely bare white wall behind Ronen, with a round paper lampshade in the upper-right corner of the screen. During their call a seven- or eight-year-old blond girl walked into the room, wearing green shorts and no shirt, peered straight at Orna with a curious look and asked Ronen something she couldn't hear. He answered her in English: 'Tell Thomas I'll be there in ten minutes, okay?' The girl looked at Orna for another moment with her big pale-blue eyes, then left the frame.

They were coming to visit in two and a half weeks, on Yom Kippur Eve. They – meaning all of them: Ronen, Ruth and her four children, one of whom was the blond, shirtless girl. Her name was Julia. They would stay for almost a month, in a house they'd rented on his parents' moshav. Ronen said he knew it wouldn't be easy for everyone, but the main purpose of the visit, from his perspective as well as from Ruth's and the kids', was to spend time with Eran and get to know him. Seeing his parents and other family was secondary. He didn't know what the right way to go about it was, which was why he wanted to talk with her now. Obviously at first they should meet together, the three of them, at least once or twice, but afterwards he would like Eran to spend a few days on the moshav with him, Ruth and their children, maybe even all of Sukkot, when he'd be on school holidays. That was why they'd decided to come now, during the High Holy Days. For Eran.

This was so like Ronen, and she told him so. Ostensibly he was coming for Eran, but he hadn't even bothered to find out if the dates worked for them before he'd bought tickets. What if they'd planned to go away on Sukkot? Hadn't it occurred to him to ask?

Ronen became defensive. 'But you're not going away, are you?' he asked.

Orna said that wasn't the point and there were lots of things that needed to be figured out and Eran needed to be prepared, they couldn't just drop this on him at short notice. 'I mean, you don't even have any idea what's going on in his life,' she added.

Ronen waited for her to calm down. He could never tolerate it when things got 'heated'. In his house everyone was calm and there were no fights. Then he said quietly, 'Orna, I understand that I've acted badly in the past few months and that everything's fallen on your shoulders, but I want to start fresh with Eran. It's important for him and for me. Think about it quietly and we'll talk before we arrive, okay? I didn't say anything to Eran about the moshav, and if it doesn't work for you I'll come to Holon every day and see him at your place, all right?'

THE FEAR THAT GRIPPED her throat was as powerful as it had been on the day she'd met Gil with his wife, and the fury was the same fury, and that made her wonder if she'd actually been angry with Ronen at the time, not with Gil. Perhaps her anxiety had been not so much because of Gil and the fact that he'd lied to her, but because of what that miserable relationship said about her fate and her life. She fell asleep late and couldn't remember her dream exactly, but she knew that the blond girl she'd seen with Ronen was in it, and that she'd been completely naked. She had to see Eran's therapist urgently, but she didn't call the next morning because she knew what he would say. Instead, she kept Ronen's looming visit to herself and felt it eating her up from inside the way acid melts away skin, until she no longer had a choice because Eran's weekly therapy session was approaching and she assumed he would say something.

She was not mistaken.

The therapist said they had to do everything slowly, 'step by step', and that of course he wanted to talk about the visit with Eran and hear what he was feeling, but that in general he saw it as 'a very positive development'. Ronen wanted to be back in Eran's life, he was willing to make a real effort and come to Israel for a relatively long period, he wanted to show Eran that there was a place for him in his new life and his new family, and that is exactly what the therapist had hoped would happen one day, and exactly what Orna had hoped for, wasn't it?

Orna found herself loathing the clinic. The parquet floor, the colourful carpets, the paintings on the walls, the books on little wooden shelves, the couch she sat opposite, covered with pillows embroidered in red and blue. The air conditioning that was always running, from April to October, as though electricity were free. How far this all was, how far all his pretty words were, from the difficulties of her life. She lost her temper: 'I don't know if I was hoping for this. Maybe you were. And I definitely didn't want it to happen this way. Do you understand what he's trying to do?'

He – Ronen – wanted Eran to fit in with his 'new family', which she was not a part of. He wanted Eran to spend several days with them in their rented house on the moshav, without her. He wanted Eran to go to sleep, perhaps in the same room, with Ruth's children, and wake up with them in the morning. Maybe Ruth would be the one to wake them all and make them breakfast and then they would go out and play without their shirts on. And where would Orna be all this time? Alone at home?

The therapist said, 'But it was clear from the moment you decided to divorce, wasn't it, Orna? It was a given. That Eran would have two families – one here with you, and one with his dad somewhere else. There is no way around that.'

But she wanted to get around it, she had to get around it, she didn't want Eran to have any family except hers. Why was that so hard to understand? Since talking to Ronen she'd had dreams in which Eran asked her if he could stay with his new family. She dreamed that he came home from the moshav and asked if he could go to Nepal with Ruth and Ronen and the kids. That he walked hand in hand with the blond girl from the screen and Orna never saw him again.

The therapist tried in vain to reassure her. 'There's no chance he'll give you up,' he said, and she heard: 'There's no chance he'll *also* give you up.' But why shouldn't he, if that's what Ronen had done? At the end of the session, the therapist said, 'Ronen has been a bad father to Eran in the past year. Very bad. But you sat here many times and told me that in the eight years prior to that he was a devoted father, and now he's trying to be a good father again and it would be wonderful for Eran if that happens, don't you agree? Parents have crises, too, and it's possible that Ronen overcame his and you have to give him a chance to make amends, for Eran's sake. We'll be cautious, Orna. We won't do anything that might hurt Eran. And don't forget that you're not alone in all this: I'm here.'

But she was alone. Completely alone. Alone with Eran in the mornings, which were more frenzied because she went to bed late and woke up in a rush, already tired. Every time she stroked his thin back under the blanket and whispered, 'Good morning, Erani,' she thought it might be one of the last times.

Eran was excited, counting the days and hours, and she could see that the excitement was bringing out something good in him. He got up quickly, got dressed and organized as if they were leaving for the airport any minute to greet Ronen rather than going to school. He did his homework diligently, without jumping up every few seconds, as if Ronen's eyes were watching him work. The notebook she'd given him turned into his preparation book for the visit, where every evening he wrote down how many days and hours were left until Dad came. She now spent all afternoon with him, as if their time were running out, and did her own work for the next day's teaching in the evening, after he went to bed. But even then she couldn't concentrate, and kept imagining Ronen and Ruth and her children in her own home, playing with Eran's toys. That was bearable compared to the moments when she imagined them all on the moshav, playing outside with a water hose, swinging in a hammock, eating supper on the lawn, with Ronen playing the guitar for them. What chance did she have against all that? And how was she supposed to survive Eran's time away without being driven mad by jealousy and anxiety?

One evening, as she was exchanging text messages with Sophie, she caught sight of Gil's last text message, the one she hadn't answered, and she suddenly felt able to reply. She wrote:

> Your absurd explanations are unconvincing, Gil. If I was a different person I would have told your wife everything long ago, and maybe I still will. I hope your marriage crumbles like you want it to, and that you won't have to lie to yourself and others any more.

9

THE NEXT TIME THEY met, it was in the morning.

Gil said it was complicated for him to see her during work hours, but Orna wasn't about to give up her evenings with Eran or tell anyone that she was meeting Gil again, and in order to go out in the evenings she would have had to get a babysitter or her mother, who would ask questions. So they arranged for Monday, her day off teaching. Half past ten. Two days before Erev Yom Kippur.

Gil was waiting in the hotel lobby, and she was almost twenty minutes late but did not send him a message. He said he hadn't booked a room because he wasn't sure if she wanted him to, and when she said, 'Then let's see if they have one,' he went over and spoke to the receptionist in a low voice. They took the small lift up to the third floor without exchanging a word, and as soon as they got to the room he went into the bathroom. She sat down on a wooden chair at the desk and waited. He seemed awkward, unsure what to say, and finally asked, 'So how are you?'

She wasn't planning to tell him anything about Ronen's visit. She remembered a brief relationship she'd once had before Ronen, with a man almost fifteen years older than her. She had been a twenty-two-year-old student, working as a flight attendant in her free time, and the man, Yigal, was a senior service manager at the airline. He was single, with a hairy body that disgusted her, and bad breath.

Gil said, 'So would you like to explain why we're meeting here? Have you decided to give me another chance or is this coming from somewhere else?' Orna replied, 'A chance for what, exactly? I've decided to let you keep lying to your wife. For now.'

They had sex without pretending that either of them wanted it or understood why. His erection was weak, barely enough to enter her, and he came quickly and outside of her, on the bed, because that was what she asked him to do. This time he didn't shower, perhaps because he was afraid to leave Orna alone in the room with his phone, which was on the bedside table, just as she remembered, underneath his brown wallet. He got dressed before she did and said, 'I don't know exactly what you want from me, Orna, but I'd be happy to see you again.' She replied with a question: 'So what are you going to tell your wife today?'

He said nothing.

When she asked, 'You haven't got divorced yet, have you?' Gil replied, 'Not yet, but it'll happen.' Orna laughed and said, 'Not because of me, I hope.' All this reminded her so much of her meetings with that man Yigal, and of the sense of disgust she had in and on her body after they had been together. She felt that everything she'd believed was behind her was now coming back, as if nothing had changed.

Then she said to Gil, 'But I have to ask you something. The flat I was in that time, where you kept inviting me – it's not really yours, is it?' Gil said it was. He'd rented it when he and Ruthi separated and had decided to keep it after he moved back home, knowing it was only going to be a temporary reconciliation.

She thought he must be lying and that he would continue to lie because he could do nothing else, but now she had an advantage, she had power, and perhaps that is what propelled her towards Gil in those days when she felt so weak ahead of Ronen's looming visit. She amused herself with the notion that she could blackmail him. Demand that he pay her a not-unreasonable sum of money, which he clearly had, in return for not telling his wife and daughters. If she asked for five thousand dollars, not fifty thousand, he would probably be tempted to give it to her because that wasn't a sum worth risking your marriage for if you didn't want it to fall apart. She might even do better: she could force Gil to pretend they were a couple when Ronen came. She could ask him to be at home with her when he visited, to play the role of her boyfriend, and then drive her to the moshav in his red Kia Sportage to pick up Eran.

She only noticed the odd coincidence – that Gil's wife was named Ruthi, just like Ronen's German wife – on the way home from the hotel. The first Ruth, the German one, had destroyed Orna's family when she'd met Ronen in Nepal, fallen in love with him, taken him away from Orna and started a new family with him. Orna would probably have to meet her soon, after having seen her only in pictures and twice on Skype when she'd quickly walked past Ronen on the screen. But for the second Ruth, Gil's Ruth, it was Orna who was in the role of 'destroyer'. That was completely different, though, because their marriage had apparently been over long ago, and she wasn't planning to start a new family with Gil.

He called her the evening after their meeting in the hotel, but she didn't answer. He called again the next day. 'I was glad to see you yesterday, Orna, even though I understand you're still angry at me,' he said. In a tone she didn't even know she possessed, she replied, 'Gil, you and I shouldn't pretend any more. Just get together and that's it. Until we get sick of that and then we'll stop. But you don't have to call me, okay? Or be nice. You and I are beyond the courtship stage.'

WHEN RONEN ARRIVED, AS soon as Yom Kippur ended, Eran was waiting for him at the window.

It was late, almost ten o'clock, but neither of them wanted to postpone the meeting. Ronen was driving his father's pick-up truck, and Eran saw him get out and rushed to unlock the front door, but he stayed in the doorway rather than running downstairs. The light came on in the stairwell, and Orna got up from the desk, where she'd been sitting with two textbooks and her computer. She stood awkwardly behind Eran.

Ronen hugged Eran and swung him up in the air. He was obviously keeping Orna at a safe or polite distance. They did not hug or kiss, and of course they did not shake hands. They stood some distance from one another, she with her hands in her pockets, he holding Eran's little hand, as if they'd come home together from a long trip. He said, 'It's good to see you, Orna, you look great,' and she said, 'Thanks.' He looked older than she remembered, his black hair a little more silver, and he also looked suddenly short – perhaps because not only was he half a metre or so shorter than her, but he was at least four inches shorter than Gil.

Eran hadn't let go of Ronen's hand yet. He took him on a tour of the flat so he could see what had changed, even though almost nothing had, except little details that only Eran noticed. Ronen walked around the home he himself had bought with Orna twelve years ago – the home that no longer belonged to him, because she had bought him out with her mother's help – and looked at it as if seeing it for the first time.

Everything in this flat used to be his, and no longer was.

At the blue Formica dining table in the kitchen he had drunk his coffee every morning for more than a decade. On the green couch in the living room he had sat every evening. In front of the old mirror in the bathroom they'd never renovated, he'd brushed his teeth twice a day. She, too, used to be his, and now she wasn't. Only Eran was still his, just as he used to be, and that was clear. Eran was the only thing Ronen wanted to take from his old home to his new family and his new life.

Orna offered Ronen coffee, and he said, 'No, thanks. I don't drink coffee any more. Just hot water.' She poured him some boiling water from the new filter system into a new mug, not one of the ones he used to drink out of, so he wouldn't think she was trying to make him nostalgic. When she took his drink to Eran's room, she found them sitting next to each other on Eran's bed. Eran was showing him the drone his grandmother had given him for his birthday and some of the model cars from his classmates. She put the mug of hot water on the floor by Ronen's feet and left to give them privacy, and also because it was too painful. While they stayed in Eran's room, she didn't know what to do with herself.

Sophie sent her a message: 'Is he there yet?'

She wrote back that he was.

'Holding up? Want me to come over?'

'Holding up for now. We'll see how it goes later.'

WHEN THEY CAME OUT of the room, hand in hand again, Ronen suggested that he put Eran to bed, but Eran said he wasn't tired yet. Ronen said, 'Then can you wait for me in your room for a minute? I want to talk to Mum.' They sat down next to each other on the living-room couch, opposite the computer, rather than at the dining table the way they used to do when they had serious talks, like the one when he first told her about Ruth.

'Something happened to me on my last trip, Orna. Something that I have no idea how to explain to you and that I never thought would happen, but it did.' That was what he'd said then.

Now he said, 'Thanks for agreeing to let me come so late. And in general thank you for letting me and Eran have all this. I really appreciate it, Orna. I'm not taking it for granted. I've been through a serious crisis in the past few months, and that's why I disappeared. I wasn't sure whether I'd done the right thing and if I was supposed to be where I was, and I thought I might come back, but I didn't want to drive you crazy, you or Eran, and in the end everything worked out for us there. I'm happy now, and I want to be part of Ran-Ran's life again, as much as possible.'

She kept her cool. All the shouts had already been shouted, all the curses hurled, all the tears shed. It was all behind her. And Eran was standing at his bedroom door listening.

Since the drive to the moshav took more than two hours, she thought Ronen would ask to sleep over, but he said, 'I want to come tomorrow, too, maybe in the afternoon, if that works for you. And after that, if you're willing, I'd like to drop by with Ruth and the kids so that Ran-Ran can meet them. If everything goes well, then I'd love to have him with us on the moshav when he's on school holidays, like we talked about. Is that okay with you? The kids really want to meet him and I think it'll be nice for him.'

She said, 'Let's start with tomorrow and see how it goes, okay? You haven't talked to him about the moshav yet, have you?' Ronen shook his head and said, 'Of course not.'

They sat silently for a while. Orna stared at Ronen's legs, folded beneath him on the couch, and he searched for her eyes. Eran's voice came from behind them: 'Mum and Dad, can I come in?'

10

RUTH WAS TALL AND broad, with pale muscular legs and thick hands and feet. Blond. Not very pretty, but with an unignorable presence, something peasant-like, earthly, perhaps maternal, although mothers in Israel look different. Her pregnant belly was large and prominent. You could understand why Ronen was attracted to her, but perhaps less so why she was attracted to him, even though he was a few years younger than her. Orna couldn't help briefly imagining Ruth walking around naked through the rooms of their house in Nepal. Eran was less interested in her than in any of the other guests. She came in last, after Ronen and the four children. Two of them were really young men, roughly fourteen and sixteen. Kurt and Thomas. There was a little boy, Peter, who was not four years old and clung to Ruth, and the girl Orna had seen on Skype, Julia, who now looked older, perhaps Eran's age. She was a curious and vibrant girl who seemed less shy than the others. Eran followed her with his gaze when she burst into the living room and looked around as if searching for something she knew was there.

Despite Orna's natural inclination to be a friendly hostess, there was not going to be any small talk between these two women, and she did not ask Ruth to sit down or offer her a drink. Ronen did not either because it was no longer his home, and Ruth stood in the corner of the living room with little Peter clinging to her knee. She didn't want to be there, that was plain to see. The older boys didn't seem to either. When Ronen introduced Ruth to Eran she smiled, held out her hand and said, in English, 'Hello, Eran, very nice to meet you,' but she did not try to interest him or talk to him any further; she certainly didn't try to win him over. She only followed him with her eyes when he was still in the living room, as though she knew this was not the time to befriend him but was planning for the days to come, when she would be able to. Ronen took Eran and Julia to Eran's room so that Eran could show her his toys, and then he called Ruth to join them. Ruth took little Peter with her, and maybe she did talk to Eran or play with him then, but Orna didn't see it.

Even though she had been prepared for the visit, Orna did not know how she was going to get through it now. Perhaps it really would have been better for them to have taken Eran from the start. They seemed awkward and cautious, apparently grasping the significance of the visit for her, and they hardly moved around, apart from Julia. But still, since there were five of them, or six with Ronen, and they whispered to each other in German, their presence in her home was aggressive and violent – more so than she had imagined in her most frightening moments. It filled the place, occupied it, turned the home into theirs and made Orna want to disappear. But she had nowhere to go. She didn't want to retreat into her bedroom and shut herself in there, that would be too exposed and humiliating, so she called Eran to the living room so as not to go near his room, which had been expropriated. He finally came after she called a few times, and she told him she was going out for half an hour to get some groceries and that he should stay with Dad – with Dad and his family, she almost said. Eran nodded and seemed completely indifferent to her leaving, as though he couldn't understand why she was even bothering to tell him. She updated Ronen, who asked if she was all right, and then she went out to the street, where she had nothing to do. She walked for a few moments and sat down on a bench.

Even her mother could have offered some comfort, but she was on her package tour of Slovenia and Croatia, and like most people in their seventies she had refused to buy a roaming package on her phone and had informed Orna she would be reachable only in the evenings, assuming the hotel had free Wi-Fi. Orna had hinted to her mother that she wasn't sure how she would get by when Ronen and his family came and took Eran to the moshav, but the tour was already paid for and couldn't be cancelled, and anyway it wouldn't have helped – on the contrary. She turned her phone on and off. A group of girls who from afar looked like her pupils walked down the street shrieking and disappeared into a building. She imagined Kurt and Thomas opening the fridge to look for something to eat, but she knew that wouldn't happen. They were too polite, and Ruth wouldn't allow them to do that, even if they wanted to. A few minutes later Ronen called, said he felt bad about her leaving and asked if they could take Eran to sightsee in Tel Aviv with them and have dinner. She had him put Eran on the phone and asked if he wanted to go. Eran said yes, but he wanted her to come too. She said she couldn't. Did he still want to go? Eran thought for a moment and then said yes. Ronen asked if she'd taken her keys and whether he should lock the door, and he promised they'd be gone in five minutes. She asked how they were getting there and he said he'd brought the van so that everyone could fit in. If it was okay with her, they'd bring Eran home at nine or ten, or whenever she said.

When she got back they were gone, and even though they hadn't left a mess she felt as if they were still there. Half-full glasses of water were in the sink, and on the living-room couch there was a red rubber ball of Eran's, and the walls spoke their German, and she had no space to move among them or air to breathe. She wanted to call Ronen and ask who Eran was sitting next to in the car. They'd probably put him between the pretty girl and Ruth. She had a few hours to kill, so she called Gil and asked him to come over. 'Are you sure?' he said, 'Isn't Eran there?' She replied, 'Come now, he'll be out till nine. He's coming home at nine.'

Gil said he would call back in a few minutes to let her know if he could make it, but when he called he said he wasn't coming.

*

IT WASN'T UNTIL THE next day, in the therapist's office, that Orna burst into tears. The therapist wanted to see her and Ronen together, before Ronen took Eran to the moshav, and he surprised her with what he told Ronen about her and his general conduct. It was the first time she'd felt he was on her side, and that he understood not only what Eran was going through but what she was too. In the first ten minutes of their session he really laid into Ronen: he told him that Eran had been through an extremely difficult year because of him, not only because of the separation but because Ronen had disappeared on him. He said that Ronen had to understand that divorcing a spouse was possible but you could not divorce your child, and that over the course of this year he'd had serious doubts about how responsible of a parent Ronen was. 'Luckily for Eran, he has a mother like Orna, who, despite her grief and her personal crisis, managed to contain his crisis too, and despite the temptation to enlist the boy in her battle against her partner – a temptation that I've seen many parents unable to resist – she took care of Eran and helped him have faith that his father would want to come back into his life one day. Most mothers I know would have behaved differently, I hope you understand that.'

Ronen looked at her. He said he completely understood. That no one knew better than he did what sort of mother Orna was to Eran.

As she had been in the first weeks after he told her about Ruth and asked for a divorce, Orna was overcome with an intense urge to hit Ronen. She wanted to put her hands on his neck and dig her nails into his flesh and squeeze. But instead she burst into tears that she could not hold back, and she left the room for a moment.

When she came back they were discussing the stay on the moshav. Ronen described the house they'd rented, right near his parents' and brother's places. He said that Eran would sleep in the same room as Ruth's little ones, Julia and Peter, but that if he preferred he could stay with his grandparents next door, in the room he knew and had slept in many times before, and that Ronen could stay there with him. They didn't have much planned other than spending time with Eran. They might go on a day trip to Masada and the Dead Sea, and another one to Jerusalem, but they could do those trips after Sukkot, too, when Eran went back to Orna's.

Eran's therapist looked at Orna: 'Is that acceptable to you?'

She said, 'We've already talked about it and that's why we're here, isn't it? You're in favour of it and you think Eran will want to go, so fine. Don't ask me if it's acceptable to me because I don't want to answer.'

The next day the therapist was supposed to meet Eran and ask him what he thought about the holiday plan, and then they would make the final decision. Yet, as if the decision had already been made, he gave Ronen his phone number at the end of the session and asked him to call with any questions or difficulties that might arise. Then he said, 'What's important for us all to clarify to Eran before the trip is that he's not moving and not changing families, but just going to spend a few days with Dad and getting to know his new family, which from now on will also be a new family for him, even if he doesn't see them very often.' He looked at Ronen and added, 'I hope you understand that this is not going to be easy for you. Eran is a very sensitive child, and even though he loves you and is very gentle, he will test you, in his own way. Particularly now, when you will be, for the first time as far as he is concerned, not only his father but the father of four other children.'

When they were at the door, the therapist asked Orna to stay for a moment, and Ronen said he would wait outside.

'Are you sure you can take it?' he wondered.

Orna almost cried again. 'I don't know. We'll live and learn, right?'

He put his hand on her shoulder for the first time since Eran had been seeing him, and came closer to her. He asked if she was planning to stay at home while Eran was gone and she said she hadn't thought about it yet, but she probably would. He hinted that perhaps she should go on holiday, just to get away and not think too much. For a moment Orna thought he was about to suggest they go away together, but he didn't. 'And maybe you should also try therapy? You haven't started anything yet, have you? I know someone excellent,' he added, after he'd let go of her shoulder and moved away.

'Maybe later,' she said. 'Let's get through this first.'

'Of course we'll get through it, Orna. Everything will be okay.'

11

AT NIGHTS, WHEN SHE gets to the hotel and logs on to the internet, Orna's mother sends pictures from Slovenia and Croatia. Lakes with sailboats, verdant mountains, bustling squares in picturesque towns. Close-ups of local delicacies served in decorative dishes on gingham tablecloths. The houses in the pictures are red, blue and yellow, like in fairy tales.

Ever since Ronen and Ruth's visit, Orna has the sense that her home has been burgled, and she acts differently in it. It has become less of a home. Perhaps that is why she asks Gil to come over when Ronen and his new family take Eran to see the Milano Circus one evening, and another time late at night, when Eran is asleep in his room. She shuts his bedroom door, warns Gil and is careful not to make any noise, but perhaps deep inside she hopes Eran will wake up and find Gil and tell Ronen that he saw a man in Mum's bedroom.

That does not happen.

Gil seems as though he is there under duress and leaves after a short while. He does not respond when she teases him with questions like, 'So what did you tell Ruthi you were doing this evening?' or 'How are Noa and Hadass? Didn't they come over for dinner today?'

She is unsure whether Gil is acquiescing to her invitations out of fear or out of pity. His discomfort is apparent; he talks very little, and there are moments when she truly feels sorry for him. They have sex in the bedroom that used to be hers and Ronen's, on the same bed, and she seems to need that. She watches herself as if from the outside while they have sex, he on his back and she on top of him, moving on his pelvis almost violently, making herself feel both disgusted and determined, as if she is trying to arouse – or anger – someone who is not in the room. It's clear to her that Gil would rather not be there, that he would prefer this relationship to be over, but he is afraid that if he ends it she will expose him to his wife and girls. Perhaps he also feels guilty. She is using him now, and even though he did the same thing to her, she feels badly about it and knows it cannot go on much longer. She asks him not to shower after they have sex because the bathroom shares a wall with Eran's room and the sound of the water would wake him, and she knows this drives Gil mad. The second time he visits her at home, she thinks he shows more interest. He looks around, examines the photos on the fridge and the South American artefacts in the living room, peeks through the blinds, stops at her computer desk. His curiosity makes her think perhaps she should have let him get close to her.

He tries to talk to her: 'Don't you want to tell me what you're going through? Something seems wrong.' And she says, 'You mean other than the fact that I'm sleeping with a married man who lied to me for six months?' Gil's face falls, and she almost regrets answering him that way, not giving him another chance. In fact, she'd never given him one to begin with – he was right, after all, when he said that she wasn't at peace with his presence in her life right from the start. But she pulls herself together and remembers that from their first date at Ha'Bima Square, long ago in early April, it had been hopeless because he'd constantly lied. When he asks, 'How long are you planning to go on this way?' she says, 'What way?' He says, 'This way, with the anger and bitterness. Why do you ask me over here?' She looks at him and smiles: 'The more interesting question is how long you could have gone on lying, isn't it? I mean, if I hadn't found out. What do you say – isn't it time we tell your wife that we're back in touch?' She didn't really mean that, and had she been asked why she said it and what she was hoping to accomplish, she wouldn't have known how to answer. Very few people had known about their relationship, and no one knows it's back on now. She isn't even planning to tell her mother. When Sophie wonders, 'Did you ever hear anything from that lawyer conman?' Orna says, 'Radio silence. And it's better that way.'

INSTEAD OF PACKING A suitcase for herself to go on holiday, she packs one for Eran. Five days' worth of clothes, mostly summer things because the forecast is predicting a heatwave, but also a pair of long trousers and one long-sleeved shirt, as the evenings can get chilly. Autumn has arrived, but there's no rain yet. Swimming trunks and goggles in case they go to the Dead Sea, which they might, or the pool, which they definitely will. Two books – *Captain Underpants* and a picture book about the history of flight – and three model cars, his most treasured ones. There are lots of toys in the rental house, so there's no need to pack too much. She asks Eran if she should put his special notebook in the suitcase and he says no, then changes his mind, perhaps because he senses her disappointment. She tells him countless times that she'll miss him and that if he writes down what they did every day, they can read it together when he gets back, if he'd like to. She says she can also keep a diary while he's gone. If she does, she thinks to herself, she'll call it 'the heartache notebook'.

In the early evening she takes Eran to the beach, which she didn't do enough over the summer. She takes his trunks out of the suitcase, and they drive to the Tel Baruch beach north of Tel Aviv. They walk on the rocks in a no-swimming area, collecting seashells and pretty stones and sea slugs in a blue bucket with sand and water. They place two glass jars with flour in them under the rocks to catch little fish. Later, when the sun starts to set and the beach empties out, they spread a towel out and wade into the warm water. The sea is dark, glimmering. The orange horizon turns blood red. The strong current pulls them towards the breaker and they hold on to each other, drift apart, then float back together. She dives and hugs his legs. When they get out of the water the wind is cold and they both shiver, and she says to Eran, 'You see? If you know how to do the right things it can be terribly cold in Israel, even on the hottest day.' She wraps him in the orange towel. They sit on the sand munching grapes and looking at the sea. Planes take off from the nearby Sde Dov airfield, thundering above them and exciting Eran, and she feels that this evening is everything she needs, that it is everything one can hope for in life. But she also knows that the fear inside her is growing deeper, and that this evening is meant to prevent Eran from forgetting her. It is meant to give him something special from her, which will be with him on the days he spends with Ronen and convince him not to want to stay with his new family.

BY THE TIME RONEN arrives at eleven the next morning, Eran is on pins and needles. She can see that he feels pure joy, unspoiled by anxiety. Ronen is businesslike. He comes up alone, takes Eran's suitcase and carries it down to the car. Then he comes back and asks Eran if he remembered to pack a toothbrush. They've already had all the 'are you sure you'll be okay?' conversations in the preceding days, and he does not say a word to Orna now. He waits in the living room while she says goodbye to Eran in his room. She reminds him over and over again that he can call her whenever he wants, that she will come and pick him up if he's uncomfortable, that if it's hard for him with the kids because of the German or for any other reason, he has Dad and also Grandma and Grandpa not far away, that she loves him and will be waiting here for him. Eran is impatient, longing to set off on his new adventure, his body taut as a coil. The minute she lets go, he wriggles out of her arms and rushes to the living room to find Ronen. She does not watch from the window as they get into the car.

And she has nothing planned for the moment after.

The hatred breaks free.

She cleans the house, goes shopping at the discount supermarket, stops at the pharmacy for painkillers, and at the nearby bookshop buys the third volume of the series she began in the summer and finished only a few days ago: *1Q84* by Haruki Murakami. She sits at the computer for a while, and at three o'clock she gets into bed with the book. How many years has it been since she was alone at home for several days? The last time was when Eran was six and Ronen took him to Lake Kinneret for two days, but then she had loads of exams to mark. For a little while she enjoys the tranquillity of the afternoon hours in bed, the grey light filtering through the window into the dark room, and the first few pages of the book. Sophie made her a list of TV series she could lie in bed and watch, but for now she prefers to read. Her eyes close and open and close again, sweet weariness relaxes her leg muscles; but very soon her thoughts wander south, to the moshav.

Ruth welcomes Eran at the front door. She hugs him. Shows him the bed he will sleep in for five nights. Helps him unpack the suitcase that Orna packed, arranges his clothes in the wardrobe. Touches his notebook.

Julia, the blond girl, barefoot and dishevelled and shirtless, waits for them to finish so she can take Eran out to the yard. In the past few nights Orna has dreamed about her twice, and in both dreams she was walking hand in hand with Eran.

The fear that he will fall in love with them, with all of them. That he will want to go to Nepal with them.

The hatred of Ronen, who hugs Ruth from behind while they watch Eran and Julia run around the garden.

SHE GETS UP TO make coffee. She calls Sophie, who's run out of ideas for keeping the kids busy in the school holidays. She asks Orna to join them on a Saturday hike at the Banias River up north with Itzik's friends from work.

She calls Gil twice, and the fact that he doesn't answer even though he's available fuels her anger. Finally he picks up and says he's in Bucharest for work. 'Are you sure you're in Bucharest?' she asks. 'If I pop over to your and Ruthi's place now, are you sure you won't be there?' He simply does not respond.

Then she says, 'Ronen is in Israel. My ex-husband. He came for a visit and I think he wants to take Eran away from me. He took him for the school holidays and I don't want to live.' Gil says, 'I'm sorry to hear that. Can I help with anything?' She laughs. She remembers how she contemplated blackmailing him so he would pretend they were a couple. Maybe she really should have done it. Demanded that he come and be with her when Ronen came over with Ruth. But she knows it's absolute nonsense, that she wouldn't have felt any better if he had been there while Ronen and his new family came, perhaps even the opposite, and that the idea was merely a manifestation of her desire to have someone, the way Ronen did, so that she would not be alone when she saw him.

'I'll come see you when I get back, Orna, all right? Tell me what he's planning and we'll see what can be done, okay? I have to go now, I'm in between work meetings here.'

At night, when the phone rings, she is sure it's Ronen and Eran again, even though they spoke two hours earlier, after Eran had showered and was ready for bed. She is disappointed to see that it's not them but Gil, and that Eran must have managed to fall asleep without her and their bedtime story after all. Gil says, 'I've been thinking, I have a great idea. Why don't you come here tomorrow or the day after? Have a holiday while Eran's gone. I'll push back my flight home, and that way you'll believe that I'm in Bucharest, won't you?'

He offers to pay for her ticket. He'll book her a room in his hotel if she doesn't want to stay in the same room. Or he can get her a different hotel if she prefers. He'll pick her up at the airport and give her a tour of the city and they can have fun together, but she can also walk around on her own if she'd like. She considers it seriously for a moment. Why not Bucharest, really? But she knows she won't go, because of the chance that Eran might want to come home early. She has to stay close to him. Besides, she needs to call off this relationship with Gil, and going to Romania with him would be the exact opposite of that. She remembers their night in the Scottish Guesthouse in Jerusalem, during the brief time when she thought something could come of it and the many hours when she knew, even then, that nothing would, even though she hadn't yet discovered that he was married. He told her then, 'You still haven't said what you think,' and when she asked, 'About what?' he said, 'About us. About me. About what's happening between us or what might happen.'

Now she says, 'And what exactly am I supposed to tell people?'

'Tell them whatever you want. You said you didn't tell anyone we were seeing each other, right? So say you're going on a little holiday alone.'

AT NIGHT ORNA DREAMS about the blond girl again, but this time Eran isn't with her. In the morning she can't remember the whole dream, only that the girl got into the swimming pool alone, and that Orna wondered if she knew how to swim because the currents in the pool were strong, and then the girl looked at her from up close, with large eyes, and said something in German that Orna couldn't understand, perhaps a warning.

An hour after she wakes up, Eran phones, just as Ronen promised, to say that he'd slept well and had had French toast with maple syrup for breakfast and they were going on a hike in the desert soon. Orna can hear in Eran's voice that he is happy.

He asks if he can stay with Dad for longer than five days.

12

GIL WASN'T WAITING FOR her at the airport. She'd turned her phone on when they landed and found a text message from a number she did not recognize: 'Held up in town with work. Take a cab to the hotel and I'll call when we finish here. If you don't have Romanian currency, you can change money at the airport.' Eran had sent her a message, too, from Ronen's phone: 'Mum hav a grate trip and a good time. We are gowing to Gran and Grampa.'

OUTSIDE THE ARRIVALS HALL everyone was smoking, and the taxi smelled of cigarette smoke. Even though she'd brought a denim jacket, she was cold. The cab driver looked Arab, didn't glance at her or try to talk with her the whole ride, and when they stopped at lights he texted on the phone attached to the windshield. They passed auto shops and gangs of stray dogs, which she'd read were common around Bucharest now. She remembered the night drives from airports to hotels in her early twenties, when she was a flight attendant, in particular one in Kiev, with two other attendants and a completely drunk driver who ran red lights the whole way, drove almost a hundred kilometres an hour inside the city and refused to let them get out. The gloomy landscapes viewed from the taxi window were unfamiliar, even though she had travelled from the airport to central Bucharest a few times, more than a decade ago. Perhaps they'd taken a different route back then. She asked herself, of course, what she was doing here. First she imagined the driver letting her off in the abandoned industrial area, near the dogs. Then, when they drove into town, she feared there would be no reservation in her name at the hotel and no rooms available. But the streets started to look familiar, perhaps because she vaguely remembered the place or perhaps because it looked like any European city, with branches of Zara and Nike and Starbucks, clean streets, tourists. They stopped outside a Parisian-looking building. Hotel Trianon, three stars. She didn't think she'd ever been there.

The front-desk clerk, who had one blue glass eye and spoke excellent English, found the reservation immediately and said, 'You'll be with us for two nights, correct?' She asked for Orna's credit card and Orna realized the room had been booked but not paid for. She was pleased about this because she'd decided on the flight that she would not let Gil pay for anything. The clerk gave her a keycard and drew blue lines under the name of the Wi-Fi network, the password and the hours breakfast was served, which were printed on the little cardboard envelope she put the key in. When Orna asked which room Gil Hamtzani was in, the clerk could not find his name in the computer. 'When is he supposed to arrive?' she asked, and Orna said, 'I think he's been here for a few days.' His name was not in the reservation system under either of the spellings they tried, and Orna said, 'Never mind, I must have been wrong.' She assumed he was staying in a different hotel for now, perhaps his usual one, where he didn't want to be seen with her, and she suddenly hoped she would manage to avoid seeing him for her entire stay.

THE HOTEL ROOM WAS much more elegant than she'd expected. There was a large bed with a maroon bedspread on ivory sheets. Very clean blue carpeting, and a dark wooden desk that was antique, or at least antique-looking. Two lamps above the bed and a lighting strip on the ceiling lit up the room in a soft golden hue, and she pulled open the blue curtains and looked out on to a quiet street named Cobălcescu. She put her little suitcase on the bed and opened it, the way she always did as soon as she checked into a hotel room, and then went back to look at the tree-lined street.

When she logged on to the Wi-Fi network she had a WhatsApp message from Sophie: 'Send pictures!' She wondered whether to take a picture of the room. So many lies she'd had to tell everyone before going away. Sophie, Eran, her mother, who was supposed to get back from Europe the next day. She told them she'd found a cheap deal for three days but not that Gil would be there and that he'd paid for her ticket. She was going alone, to clear her head and get some rest, and mostly to get away from the empty house and from everything that was happening with Ronen and Eran. Sophie thought it was an excellent idea. She was only sorry she couldn't join Orna, because Itzik had sprained a muscle on their hike and couldn't be alone with the kids. Orna sent her a photo of the room and one of the quiet street, framed by the open blue curtains, and Sophie immediately responded with a picture of a pile of dirty dishes in the sink.

Maybe she had done the right thing.

She wouldn't wait for Gil. In fact, she would make every effort to avoid him. The fact that he'd bought her the ticket could be ignored – she could think about that as compensation, or simply pay him back in Israel. She knew the ticket hadn't been cheap, a little over 450 euros, but still she decided she would pay him back in full, and the decision liberated her. She remembered that she used to know how to find her way around foreign or semi-foreign cities with her eyes closed and with no map. A sense of direction based on a natural attraction to beauty – that was how she used to think of it. It had been honed over dozens of one-night stays in cities all over the world, always leading her to the most attractive streets, the most charming squares and the loveliest cafés. Now, with Google Maps and the Bucharest tourist app, it should be much easier, but she decided not to use them. Without planning a route, she left the hotel, turned right, then right again, and found herself on a main road that she felt she should stay on, and after three or four minutes she realized she was correct and that she was approaching the old city.

It was five o'clock and the sky was cloudy and leaden, as if it were getting dark. She remembered Bucharest being dirtier and poorer, and was surprised to see hotels with grand casinos and signs in Hebrew asking guests to deposit their passports at the front desk. At first she didn't take pictures because she preferred to photograph things with her eyes and her memory, or in fact with her soul, as Ronen used to say. But when she remembered that line of his she took her phone out and snapped pictures to show Eran when she got home. She didn't look for a fine-dining restaurant but for street food, as she always used to on her short trips – not just to save money, but also because they served the simplest, tastiest dishes. She found a stall selling rolled pastries filled with soft cheese, a sort of Romanian version of the Georgian *khinkali* or *bourekas* from back home.

At eight o'clock she wanted to go back to her room to Skype with Eran before he went to bed. She stopped at a souvenir shop in the old city and bought him a traditional wooden sword, a colourful flute and a white T-shirt with a picture of Dracula, which she wasn't sure she would give him because it was a little scary. As she approached the hotel, she spotted Gil waiting outside. He looked tense, standing there in a grey suit she'd never seen him wearing in Israel, looking around. 'You're full of surprises, even abroad,' she said. He said he was sorry, his work meetings had taken much longer than he'd expected, and he was happy she'd found the hotel. He asked how her room was.

'The room's nice,' she said. 'Aren't you staying in this hotel after all?'

As far as she was concerned, this trip was already over and had not been in vain after all: all she'd needed was the flight and checking into the hotel and the short walk around the streets of Bucharest, which had proved to her that her sense of direction wasn't lost and she could still find her way around. Now she was ready to fly home without even spending the night, just like she used to do.

Gil said he hadn't been at this hotel before but a local lawyer friend had recommended it. He was staying on the other side of town, closer to the government offices where he had most of his meetings. He wanted to find out if she liked her room before he got one for himself, and he was wondering if she wanted him to get a separate room or if she preferred that they sleep in the same room. She said, 'How do you usually do things with the girls you bring here?' But then she felt angry at herself for allowing him to spoil her mood.

Gil didn't smile this time. She said she'd rather he get his own room and that she wanted to pay him back for the flight. The whole thing about the hotel on the other side of town was absurd, and now she didn't believe his stories about what he was doing in Bucharest either. She realized she knew nothing about his work, and assumed he was probably connected to the casinos with Hebrew signs that she'd seen. Why would a lawyer have to go to Bucharest so often to get Romanian passports for Israelis? Anyway, she could no longer be bothered with the hide-and-seek games and his lies, and she wanted to talk to Eran. She made up her mind not to see Gil any more.

He asked if she wanted to go out for something to eat, and she said she had to go up to her room to make a phone call and that he should probably call his wife. She said perhaps they could meet later if she wasn't too tired, although she knew she was going to crawl into bed and simply fall asleep. When she walked into the hotel and realized he wasn't following her in, she asked, 'Oh, is that so no one sees us going in together? But no one knows you here, do they?' Gil replied, 'Orna, could you stop? I'm coming in soon. A courier is supposed to drop off some documents for me.' But she had the feeling he realized she'd lost interest and would simply wait for her to disappear into the hotel and then vanish from her life. He didn't even have a suitcase. And she knew that when they got back to Israel she would have the strength, this time, to cut off this morbid relationship once and for all.

Despite the way she'd teased him, she felt no real insult or anger at his lies, not even a sense of self-loathing. There was a slight fear, because she realized she knew much less about him than she'd thought. But she felt free, not just of Gil, and more confident in her ability to get along on her own, to cope with whatever life threw at her. She could even handle Eran's request to spend more time with Ronen or to go to live with him and his new family in Nepal. She would simply tell him: No, you can't move to Nepal because you are my son, and no one will take better care of you than I will. Because I'm not giving you up and you know you can't give me up, and even if you don't know that now, you'll understand it when you're older.

She called Eran on Skype as soon as she got into her room. When Ronen answered, he said, 'You look good, Orna. Are you having fun? How's Bucharest?' She replied, 'Wild. How's Eran?'

He was still in the shower because they'd just got back from the pool. Ronen said he'd be out in a minute, and even though she didn't ask, she knew with certainty that Eran was showering with Julia and that Ruth was helping them both wash. A few minutes later they appeared on the screen together: Julia, wearing nothing but a pair of orange panties, stood opposite the camera, then Eran ran over behind her, wrapped in a white towel with his straight brown hair sopping wet.

She asked Ronen to leave her alone with Eran and he took Julia by the hand and left the room. 'How are you, my love? I miss you so much,' she said. And he answered, 'I'm fine, Mum. Where are you?'

She told him again that she'd taken a Boeing 737 with two engines to the capital of a country called Romania, and that she was in her hotel room after walking around the city and eating a delicious dinner and buying him presents. 'Do you want to see my room?' But Eran wanted to see the gifts, and when she took the wooden sword and the T-shirt out of the black plastic bag and held them up for him, she thought he looked pleased. 'Ran-Ran, do you still feel good with Dad?'

'Yes. Have you decided if I can stay for more than five days?'

'I've decided that you can't, my boy. I miss you too much, and I won't manage for more than five days without you. But Dad will come to visit us lots more before they leave.'

That was how it always was between then.

Short conversations, without many words.

What was important was all the rest – communicating with their eyes, or with their bodies getting closer and farther away from each other, like on that evening in the dark sea that had swept them apart and back together. Eran nodded and she could see that he wasn't angry about her refusal. Perhaps it even made him happy. 'You don't want to tell me more about your day right now, do you? Are you too tired?' she asked.

'It was fun at the pool. We're having schnitzel for dinner.'

'Are you writing in your notebook, like you promised? So you can read me everything when we meet?'

He hadn't written anything yet.

Then she asked him to blow her a kiss through the computer and she caught it and he pressed the button that made her vanish from the screen.

AT FOUR MINUTES TO nine there was a knock on the door. She was still dressed, even though she knew for sure that she would not go out to eat but would shower and put on her pyjamas and go to bed. Gil had called eight or nine times, and she'd ignored his calls, hoping he would stop, but something in his numerous attempts and the fact that he didn't hang up even after ten rings bothered her and made her think he wasn't going to give up on dinner.

She opened the door without knowing it was Gil, and he marched in and put his soft hand over her mouth. He shut the door behind him and pushed her to the bed before she realized what was happening, with a strength she'd never before felt in him. He knocked her on to the bed so that her face was crushed in the pillow and her mouth was blocked, then he pulled her arms behind her back and put his knee on her hands. She felt him tying her wrists with fabric, and after her hands were secured he tied a towel around her mouth.

Orna fought him with her legs and back, tried to push him off and kick him with her heels, but he dug his knee deeper into her back until she thought her spine was going to break, and he pushed her face harder into the pillow until she could feel the air running out. In the seconds that passed before she lost consciousness, she thought he wanted to hurt her: it wasn't possible that he was trying to kill her, even though that was how it seemed. The pain in her back was unbearable. She shouted, 'What are you doing, Gil?!' but her voice went unheard.

WHEN SHE CAME TO, her hands were still tied and her mouth gagged, and she was lying on the bed in the same position. Her back hurt. She wasn't sure how much time had gone by, but the room was almost completely dark, as if several hours had passed. Was it the middle of the night? Gil noticed her moving and turned to her, and she saw that he was sitting on the bed next to her, holding her phone. The TV threw off colourful lights into the black space of the room.

She still didn't understand what he wanted, and he said to her quietly, 'What's the code for your phone?' as if he'd forgotten that he'd gagged her with a towel. When she tried to roll over and lie on her arms and her aching back, he turned her back on to her stomach and said, 'Please signal to me with your fingers.'

And that was all he said.

After that, for the next few minutes, he did not say a word and did not make a sound. He did some things on her phone that she could not see, but in the light coming from the screen she noticed that he had rubber gloves on. And she realized he was going to try to kill her. He must be deleting the messages he'd sent her, as if the murder itself had already been committed and all that was left for him to do now was cover his tracks. But she was still alive. She tried to move around on the bed and roll off it, and he got up and dug his knee into the middle of her back again while he kept working on the phone.

These are not my final moments, she thought. This is not the end. She also thought: I will not see Eran again. Is this why he brought me to Romania? Was it all part of a plan? Isn't anyone going to catch him? She knew he would only be caught if she could stay alive, because she hadn't told anyone they were in touch, hadn't mentioned him to anyone for months, and no one knew she'd come here to see him. But he'd booked her plane ticket and that had to be on record somewhere, and he'd also booked the hotel, unless he'd planned all this ahead of time and had made the reservations under fictitious names. She remembered that she'd left the curtains open, as she always did, so that the view would be in her sight at all times, but she saw he'd drawn them shut. She thought about the front-desk clerk with the glass eye, who'd looked for 'Gil Hamtzani' a few hours ago in the hotel computer. Would she remember his name tomorrow? But tomorrow was not the end.

And then, during one of her attempts to turn around and fall off the bed, Orna saw the white cord and she realized.

No one would catch him.

It was a long, white electrical cable, at the end of which was a block with three sockets. A loop had been tied on the other end, and she realized he was going to kill her with that cable and stage her death as a suicide. He was going to tighten the loop around her neck and hang the cable from the curtain rod or some other place near the ceiling. And disappear. Leave the room under cover of darkness and go back to his room, if he had one, or leave the hotel, if he was staying somewhere else. Fly back to Israel without knowing anything about the woman he'd never met who had committed suicide in a hotel room in Bucharest, a woman whose murderer no one would look for, because the Romanian police would declare it a suicide, and her relatives would also accept that she might have committed suicide because of her grief over Ronen and Eran. And it would work out well for Ronen, because now Eran would be his and no one would put obstacles in his path when he wanted to take him to Nepal. Was he sending goodbye messages in her name from her phone now? Perhaps he was writing a farewell note from her to Eran? Eran, Eran, Eran – only Eran.

She did not stop talking in her head, even though no one could hear her.

And Gil had still not said a word.

He got up and put her phone down on the desk, then came closer and put the pillow over her head again. The air would run out again. She wanted to think only of Eran, Eran, Eran, but she saw him with Julia, who looked back at her the way she had from the computer screen, wearing the orange panties.

This couldn't be the end.

No one would ever catch him.

But I didn't commit suicide, I would never leave you. Someone must know that. Someone knows. That is not my farewell letter. You know. You. You. You.

Perhaps it is not the end after all.

How could it be that I'm dying and Eran's body is so far away from mine?

Two

I

NACHUM DIED ON THE twenty-fifth of December, the birthday of the Son of God.

Four days earlier he'd woken up in the middle of the night unable to breathe. An ambulance took him to hospital, and from that moment on they no longer needed Emilia. Nurses and doctors cared for Nachum. His children came to the hospital and sat outside his room, and Emilia guessed from their facial expressions and what little they said to one another in Hebrew that he was going to die.

She sat next to them in the corridor, but felt uncomfortable, so she took the lift to the ground floor and went out into the cold open air of the hospital plaza. When she returned, a Russian-speaking nurse asked if she was Nachum's caregiver, and when Emilia said she was, the nurse told her she should start looking for a new job. The doctors had put Nachum to sleep and hooked him up to a respirator and he would not last more than another two or three days. All his systems were in shutting down.

'How old was he?' the nurse asked, as if Nachum were already in heaven.

Emilia said, 'Eighty-four.'

'How many years have you been caring for him?'

Two years.

Since the day she came to Israel.

During the first year he got around with a walker, and he talked, and he made Emilia a notebook with letters and words so that she could learn Hebrew. But in the last few months he no longer talked or walked, and she would take him out in a wheelchair so that he wouldn't be cooped up at home all day. He would sit in the wheelchair in the sun with his eyes shut, for an hour or two, depending on the weather. His head would droop on his chest as if he'd fallen asleep. Sometimes his eyes would open suddenly and he would look around, perhaps startled, afraid he was alone, until he saw Emilia next to him and calmed down. The sun would light up his face. She would sit next to him on a bench under a tree.

She didn't know much about him, except what his wife, Esther, had told her: he had been a paediatrician, he'd been born in the city of Linz in Austria, he'd had his first stroke four years ago, at eighty, and had been otherwise healthy. Before the stroke he'd enjoyed playing with his granddaughters, but wished he had grandsons. Since retiring as a doctor his hobbies included writing a book about treating children's diseases, and building wooden toys with little engines, like steam trains or merry-go-rounds, neither of which he was still doing by the time Emilia arrived.

At midday, Nachum's older daughter suggested that her mother go home to rest, because there was no point in her waiting around. She asked Emilia to go with her.

Emilia offered to cook, but Esther didn't want to eat, and Emilia had nothing else to do. She sat in her room, the room she would have to leave in a few days. An almost empty room, with walls of faded white, a narrow bed, a wardrobe, a little television on a low table and a transistor radio.

At the funeral held in the cemetery in Petah Tikva, no one came up to console Emilia.

NACHUM AND ESTHER'S FOUR children were just as courteous as they'd been since she'd started working for them. They told her she could stay in the little room until she found new work and a new bed. She offered to help during the shiva – she could cook, serve food, wash dishes, clean the living room and the bathroom at the end of the day – but they refused. They said she wasn't a maid, that she'd been there solely to take care of Dad, and that in any case the whole family would help with the shiva. Guests brought platters of baked goods and biscuits, and some relatives came with pots of soup or other dishes. Women washed dishes in the kitchen. Emilia had no reason to be there, so she came back to her little room only at night, because for now she had nowhere else to sleep. She left at half past seven every morning, after breakfast with Esther and before visitors arrived to offer their condolences, and returned at ten or eleven at night, when everyone had left and the flat was dark. She began looking for new work through the employment agency that had brought her to Israel, in classified ads in the Russian newspapers, and by asking the few other caregivers she knew. She tried to learn Hebrew again, using the notebook Nachum had made for her, but as with her previous attempts, she felt that she couldn't even cross the barrier of the peculiar shapes, even now, when it was so critical.

Until a few months ago she'd hoped the Hebrew was growing inside her like a tree, that the characters were its trunk and the words were the leaves or fruits. But now her hope was fading, as though it had died with Nachum or remained in the little room she was about to leave.

Nachum's family wrote a short recommendation letter for Emilia in Hebrew and told her in English what it said: that she was a trustworthy, diligent worker, that she had taken care of their father like a devoted nurse or a mother caring for her baby. A man who came for the shiva heard them praising her and asked if Emilia would be willing to move to Haifa to take care of someone's mother, but it turned out that without very good Hebrew she would not be able to do it.

Emilia sat on the bench under the tree where she used to sit with Nachum, and tried to work out whether she should go back to Riga. The days were cold, which reminded her of things she had forgotten. The thought of moving in with a different family frightened her.

But two days after the shiva ended, a woman named Nurit from the agency told her they'd found her a job with a new old lady in a nursing home in Bat Yam, just south of Tel Aviv. It was a part-time job, three days a week, no overnights. Nurit said that Emilia would have to find somewhere to live until they decided if the job would become full-time and include room and board, so she started to look for a flat to rent in Bat Yam before she'd figured out whether she would stay in Israel.

When Emilia packed her two suitcases and said goodbye, Esther asked what was in the flat she'd rented. She said Emilia could take anything she needed from the little room, including the television and the radio. Emilia debated whether or not to take them, and in the end she said no. Esther asked, 'Do you have pots and pans there? Kitchenware?' But Emilia would only agree to take the mug she used for coffee in the mornings. Esther asked her not to disappear: 'You may not know this, Emilia, but it wasn't just Nachum – I've also grown attached to you.' Emilia promised to visit.

She took the lift in which she used to take Nachum down to the garden in his wheelchair, and she passed the bench she used to sit on next to him and the tree that had protected them both from the sun and the rain.

She was certain it was the last time she would see either of them.

2

ESTHER PHONED ALMOST A month later.

Tuesday, early February. She called in the morning, while Emilia was at the nursing home in Bat Yam with Adina, the new lady. Emilia answered the phone and whispered that she couldn't talk and would call Esther back later. When Adina took her afternoon nap, Emilia stepped out on to the balcony. Esther's voice made her happy. She asked in Hebrew, 'How are you, Emilia?' and Emilia was going to apologize for not being in touch, but Esther said, 'Where have you been, Emilia? You said you wouldn't disappear but you did. Are you working hard? Do you not have time to come and visit? You don't know how difficult it is for me at home without Nachum.'

Esther's voice brought back to Emilia the sight of the little room she'd left, with the kids' bed she'd slept on for two years and the greying walls. She told Esther in English, 'On Thursday I have day off and I can visit you in morning. You will be home?' Esther answered in Hebrew, 'I'm home all day. Today I might go to the hairdresser. But call before you come so I can get ready.' It was clear from her voice that she did not want to end the conversation when she said to Emilia, 'But tell me how you are – are you happy there? Do they treat you well?'

ON THURSDAY SHE WENT to visit Esther, as promised.

On the bench under the tree outside the building a young woman sat next to a pram. Emilia remembered her: the neighbour from the ground floor, the wife of the tall man who'd helped her push Nachum's wheelchair into the lift when one of the wheels got stuck. When Emilia left, the woman had been pregnant, with an enormous belly. She greeted Emilia with a smile; perhaps she remembered her, even though they'd never spoken.

Esther opened the door in her brown nightgown, even though it was half past eleven and Emilia had called at ten o'clock to remind her that she was coming. Her grey hair was dishevelled, as if she hadn't brushed it since Nachum died. They hugged, and Esther asked, 'What is this, Emilia? Why are you so thin?'

On the coffee table there was a tray with biscuits on a little dish and a shop-bought marble cake. Nachum's wheelchair was gone, and the blinds on the window facing the garden were shuttered. But the smell of the flat was still the same smell that had been so foreign in the first few weeks and had since become the smell of home: it was Nachum's body odour and medication, Esther's lotions, the old walls and the decomposing wood in some of the kitchen cupboards. Esther asked Emilia if she wanted tea or coffee, and when Emilia offered to make it herself for them both, Esther said, 'Of course not, you sit down. Today you are a guest.' She went to the kitchen and Emilia stayed alone and did not know how to be a guest in a flat that up until a month ago was both her home and her place of employment.

When Esther came back with the cups she started talking immediately. And she talked as if she hadn't spoken to anyone for weeks. She told Emilia that she was still going to the pool three times a week but didn't have the strength to swim so she only did aerobics. She said that the kids visited but not much, and she felt she was still recovering from the shiva, with all the visitors. Sometimes the kids' friends came in the evening and stayed late, and one couldn't ask them to leave, even though she was used to going to bed early.

Seeing that Emilia wasn't eating anything, Esther asked again why she looked so thin and if she'd stopped eating. Before Emilia could answer, Esther added, 'I'm so sad that you left, Emilia. If it were up to me I would have kept you, but I'm still strong, what can you do? Maybe if you're in Israel when I get sick you'll come and care for me. You'll stay here, won't you? You're not going back home?'

Emilia said she wasn't, even though her thoughts of returning to Riga were becoming more frequent.

When she told Esther that the flat looked neater, Esther said, 'Should I tell you why? It's because I started removing his things. Very slowly, because I don't have the strength. First of all the books. Every day I put two or three books out in the stairwell, and the neighbours take them or throw them away for me. Today I put out his old stereo, remember? Didn't you see it outside?'

She did not invite Emilia to see the little room that used to be hers, and Emilia did not ask. And they hardly mentioned Nachum beyond the conversation about his belongings. Esther asked how Emilia was getting along in her new job, and Emilia did not tell her so as not to sadden her or complain. She changed the topic and told Esther that she was looking for extra work to cover her rent, and Esther asked, 'Would you like me to ask the old people around the neighbourhood or at the pool? How many free days do you have?' Emilia said she had two, Saturdays and Thursdays, and also weekends, if necessary. She could work early in the morning, as soon as the buses started running from Bat Yam, all the way to the evening. She told Esther that a caregiver she'd met in the dining room at the nursing home had offered her a job cleaning lobbies or flats or offices on her free days. As she talked she constantly looked for Nachum, as if he might still be there; she often had trouble believing he wasn't. She did not tell Esther that she saw Nachum when she was alone in her flat in Bat Yam or at the nursing home, and that she sensed he was trying to tell her something but was unable to. The first time she saw him it was just a flash, among the dozens of old people in the dining room, and his face scared her – his eyes were sunken and his skin almost translucent – but since then she'd grown accustomed to his deathly pallor, and he no longer frightened her.

Esther said, 'Why should you do cleaning work, Emilia? I don't think that's a good idea. Wouldn't it be better for you to take care of someone else? You do it so well. Besides, are you allowed to do that?'

Emilia said that the caregiver she'd met in the dining room had said it was good work because you could do it for cash, without permits and without telling the agency. If she didn't want to get into trouble she could also consult a lawyer and find out how to change the work permit she'd been issued from the Ministry of the Interior so that it would be legal. Esther said, 'You know what? Why don't you ask Gil? You know he's a lawyer, right? I'm almost positive he works with these matters too. You remember Gil, don't you? He'd be happy to help you. I'll feel better if you do it properly, because otherwise they could deport you. You know what they do here now because of the blacks, right?'

Esther went to her bedroom and came back with her mobile phone to call Gil right then and there, but he didn't answer, and she said, 'Well, he never picks up when I call.' She wrote down his number on a piece of paper for Emilia. Then she asked Emilia to stay for lunch and insisted, even when Emilia refused because she could see that the visit was tiring Esther since she had to speak in English part of the time.

They had lunch in the kitchen, at the table where they used to drink coffee every morning. And they hardly spoke during the meal. Emilia asked Esther who cooked for her and Esther replied that she'd started cooking a little again, and she asked if the soup was all right. She kept saying to Emilia, 'If I hear about any work here, I'll tell you,' and she added at least twice, 'Don't forget to phone Gil. I'm sure he'll be nice to *you*.'

When they said goodbye she urged Emilia to visit again, but Emilia sensed that this time Esther would not phone.

3

THIS IS WHAT EMILIA tried to hide from Esther, and believes she is successfully hiding from others: She is sinking. She needs a hand to reach out and stop her from drowning. Or at least a sign that help is on the way.

Her work at the nursing home in Bat Yam is completely different than it was with Nachum. The home is made up of two tall towers that are like two hives of old people and caregivers, right near the beach. Emilia is not alone. She meets caregivers, men and women, from Ukraine, Bulgaria, Thailand, Colombia, Romania, Poland, Moldavia and the Philippines. She meets them in the lift, in the sky-blue-carpeted hallways, in the lobby, in the dining room that has yet to be renovated and is dank and dark, and in the courtyard. Here and there conversations evolve. Some of the caregivers live in the home with their patients and some in rented rooms like Emilia's. In little groups or alone. Some of them have families and children in Israel, some have families in the countries they come from. The main topic of their brief conversations is money. They are all looking for extra income. Many work two jobs. Emilia is asked, 'How long have you been in Israel?' 'Which agency brought you?' 'How long are you planning to stay?' Over and over again. The questions she asks herself are much more desperate.

The lady she takes care of, Adina, is ninety-two. She speaks very little English. She can say basic words like *come* or *go out* or *clean*, but she understands more. She has a daughter, Hava, who is about sixty, and judging by the framed photographs on a shelf in her room she might have had a son, too, who died. And five grandchildren, one of whom is doing his military service.

On the first day at work Hava told Emilia that her mother is no longer completely lucid. There are days when she knows what's going on, and days when she knows less. Until two years ago she was completely independent, and for the past two years an Israeli woman had come twice a week to clean and do her laundry and shopping. Now things are deteriorating. Adina needs supervision for most of the day and night. She cannot be left alone for more than two or three hours during the day, while she's watching TV. So Hava comes on Saturdays and Thursdays and weekends, and the rest of the week will be Emilia's. If the social worker determines that Adina needs constant care, they can hire Emilia full-time, although there is also the possibility of moving her into the nursing ward. If Emilia wants to stay she will have to improve her Hebrew, because otherwise it will be very difficult to spend twenty-four hours a day with Adina, even though most of the staff at the home speak English and can help.

Hava is less courteous than Nachum's children. More suspicious. And her interactions with Adina are unpleasant. There is something violent about her movements and her expression when she touches Adina to help her get up from her seat or sit down on the old couch in the tiny living room, and in the way she instructs Emilia about how to do things with her mother.

Emilia learns quickly. She walks Adina to the dining room and serves her a peeled hard-boiled egg, a slice of white bread, some cut-up vegetables and a spoonful of cottage cheese. After breakfast they go for a walk in the lobby and the garden. If it isn't raining they go to the boardwalk opposite the home. Adina asks to sit far away from the building, to avoid conversations with the other residents, and she watches the passers-by with a focused look, as if searching for someone. Then Emilia takes Adina back up to her room on the seventh floor and does various jobs. She goes out to buy medication or food if needed, cleans the room, does the laundry. They communicate with Emilia's meagre Hebrew and Adina's limited English, but mostly with hand signals. Most of the time Adina is sullen. She raises her voice. She says things Emilia is happy that she cannot understand.

After lunch, which they eat with everyone in the dining room, Adina has a rest and usually falls asleep. In the afternoons they are supposed to go to a lecture in the auditorium or play cards in the basement, but sometimes they stay in and Adina watches television, and after dinner Emilia helps her shower.

She leaves after eight, when Adina is almost asleep. Above her bed is an emergency call button and the home has on-call staff who will come if she presses it. Emilia locks the door with the key Hava gave her. Adina barely responds when Emilia tells her she's leaving and when she arrives again in the morning.

WITH NACHUM, EVEN THOUGH in the last year he was unable to speak, it was different. Especially in the moments when he would suddenly open his eyes, anxiously search for Emilia, give her a surprised look and then calmly close his eyes again. With Adina everything is the opposite. Emilia knows that Adina doesn't want her there and that any other caregiver could do the job better than her. She tells herself this cannot be the reason why she is here, so far away from where she was born. There must be a different reason, something she does not yet understand and has to find, and if she does not find it she must go back to Riga, even though no one is waiting for her there either.

Emilia does not give up. Each day begins with the hope that something good will happen.

At nights she has trouble falling asleep, because the flat she rents is on a main road and there is noise from the traffic all night, and also because of the cold. She knows she may have to move again soon, to Adina's home, but even so she goes to a homeware shop on Balfour Street and buys some dishes she likes, a frying pan, two colourful towels and a blanket. She spends a lot of time cleaning the flat, which was previously rented by three Georgian workers who never cleaned it. In the evenings she has a ten-minute walk back from the nursing home. She stops at the supermarket for tomatoes, cucumbers, lemons, a few apples and bottles of mineral water, because the tap water is cloudy, and that is all she eats at home. She stops buying bread. There is no mirror in the flat, and Emilia decides she doesn't need one, but in the mirrors at the nursing home she can see that she is losing weight.

She makes herself a cup of very sweet tea in the evening, the way her mother used to make it for her, and she misses Riga – or rather, not Riga but the home she grew up in and the hours when she used to wait alone for her father to come home from work, always before Mother did. Emilia would lay the table with two plates, one for her father and one for herself, and next to each of them she would place a knife, fork and spoon. In the middle of the table she would put a brown basket with half a loaf of bread left over from breakfast. The deep plates were decorated with storks and geese in yellow and black. Emilia was not allowed to turn on the stove, so her father would heat up the food when he got home for his lunch break. Emilia would clear the dishes after lunch and wash them in cold water in the kitchen sink.

On the floor above her flat in Bat Yam lives an elderly couple, and since Emilia keeps her windows open to the cold air and evening smells, she can hear the man shouting at his wife in Hebrew and the wife answering. Most of the time she feels fine with her decision not to take the television or radio from Esther, because her flat seems more and more like a sort of cavern, a place where she must prepare herself. It is fourteen square metres, and it's unclear how the Georgians who lived there managed to fit in three mattresses. But precisely because Emilia has no television or radio, the sounds she happens to hear on the bus or from Adina's television can send chills down her spine, as do voices that drift through the open window, because each of them might be saying something that Emilia needs to hear. A voice to guide her. A sign.

And it's possible that it has already come.

IT HAPPENED WHEN A Filipina caregiver named Jennifer pinned a sign on the noticeboard next to the lift, inviting believers to Mass on Ash Wednesday, which marks the beginning of the forty days of Lent. Emilia saw the Filipina putting up the sign and asked her what language the Mass would be held in, and the Filipina said English. She couldn't go because she worked on Wednesdays, but she realized that she might have unwittingly started Lent by deciding to give up television and radio, and with her new diet.

On her forty-sixth birthday, which was near the end of January and which no one but her celebrated, she visited the church for the first time. She'd copied down the address from the Filipina's notice. She took the bus to Jaffa but realized she could have walked all the way along the beach, because her flat was no more than three kilometres away. And that, too, was a signal.

She did not know much about what one was supposed to do in

church, apart from what everyone knows. She did not cross herself or kneel in front of the marble statue of the Son of God when she entered the large hall for the first time. As a child, Emilia had not gone to church much because her father did not believe in the Son of God back then, while her mother, who did seem to have believed, went infrequently and usually without Emilia, so as not to anger Father. But on the bus to Jaffa, Emilia remembered visiting St Peter, in the old city of Riga, as a little girl, with her Aunt Stefka, her mother's older sister. Stefka had come to live with them when Emilia's mother fell ill, and she and Emilia were supposed to pray together for her mother to get well. Emilia not only prayed for good health but also asked that her mother not keep suffering. When she died, less than a week later, Emilia felt guilty and did not tell anyone about her secret prayer.

The Mass in Jaffa was held in Polish, and Emilia sat on a wooden pew in the back and listened to the prayers without understanding much. The priest's voice echoed through the empty space like music.

Before leaving, she bought a candle and lit it from the flame of one of the other candles that burned near the baptism font, and when she put her candle next to the others and inhaled the smell of burning wax, she thought about Nachum and Esther, and also about her mother and her father, who only a few weeks before his sudden death had started talking to her about the Son of God.

Now she goes to the church in Jaffa every Sunday, to the exact same Mass in a language she cannot understand. She discovers that the Jaffa church is also named for St Peter, like the ancient one in

Riga, and she begins to recognize the worshippers. She thinks the young priest recognizes her too. Every Sunday she allows herself to get closer to him, to sit on a pew nearer the front, to move her lips in front of him.

She still does not dare talk to him, even though she wants to and knows she will.

She does not understand most of the words in the prayers, even though the sounds of some of them are close to the sounds of her own language. But as the days go by, she begins to feel that perhaps He is not guiding her in a language of words and letters but in a different language, the language of things, the language of events and occurrences that no notebook can teach her, and that in order to understand she must open all the windows and allow things to enter.

And that is exactly what she tries to do.

After her visit with Esther, she takes the bus back to Bat Yam and gets off on Balfour Street, goes into the homeware shop and buys an embroidered tablecloth, a plastic dish rack and a little basket for baked goods or fruit. That evening she finds in the pocket of her trousers the piece of paper with Gil's phone number, and she calls him, because she has to find more work and make more money.

In her notebook, where she copies down Hebrew words and short sentences that she sees on signs and tries to memorize, is the name of the street where the church is located, names of the two streets that lead to the church from the bus stop and Emilia's own name, in Hebrew, drawn in pencil, as though it were composed not of letters but of pictures.

She visits the cemetery where Nachum is buried and copies the inscription on his grave into her notebook.

'Our beloved grandfather, father and husband.'

'Salt of the earth, a pioneer and a children's doctor.'

'May his soul be bound in the eternity of life.'

When Emilia places a large bouquet of flowers that she bought outside the cemetery on his grave, she sees Nachum not far away, among the other graves, watching her with eyes that turn slowly black.

4

HER FIRST MEETING WITH Gil was on a Sunday, near the end of February. Still winter.

A few days earlier the bad news had come. When Emilia opened the door to Adina's room, she'd found her daughter, Hava, organizing the wardrobe. Hava asked if Nurit from the agency had spoken with her, and when Emilia said no, she told her the National Insurance had finally authorized a full-time caregiver for Adina and she could move into the nursing home on the first of March.

She took Emilia to Adina's bedroom. The wardrobe was open and clothes and faded towels were arranged on the bed in tall piles, and Hava asked if one drawer and three shelves would be enough. She said Adina had spare sheets and blankets, and if there was anything else Emilia needed, she should make a list. Hava would see what she had at her place, and whatever they still needed she'd get hold of.

Adina sat on the couch in the tiny living room, and even though she did not follow their whole conversation, she apparently understood the preparations her daughter was making. She yelled at Hava in Hebrew that she didn't want Emilia to live with her, she didn't need her and Emilia was stealing money from her. Emilia was horrified, even though Hava told her in English to ignore Adina. 'Do you understand what she's saying?' Hava asked. 'She thinks everyone steals from her. Mostly me and my husband and the kids. As if she even has anything left worth stealing. All she did her whole life was waste money. Now there's nothing left and I have to spend my own money on her.'

EVEN THOUGH SHE NO longer needed legal counsel, Emilia did not cancel the meeting with Gil.

She woke up early, when it was still dark outside. She drank her coffee in the kitchen by the open window, with the lamp on. She did not have many such mornings left. In the little basket from the homeware shop, which she'd placed on the embroidered tablecloth in the middle of the table, were a few lemons and apples. During a brief lull in the traffic outside, Emilia heard a woman walking by quickly in high heels. She told herself these changes were for the best; her salary would be higher, and she wouldn't have to pay rent. She couldn't have stayed in this flat for much longer anyway because she didn't have enough money. Yet still she felt that moving to the nursing home would be even harder than leaving Nachum and Esther's home.

The number 42 bus took her from Bat Yam to Ramat Gan. She got on at the beginning of the route, and so she found a seat at the back, next to a steamy window. She wore the same grey jeans and grey T-shirt she always wore, and large sunglasses. Since she'd lost so much weight, the clothes hung loose on her body, but she couldn't imagine herself wearing anything else, nor could she afford new clothes now. In a plastic bag she had a long black purse and an old mobile phone.

Emilia held the plastic bag on her lap.

The passengers in the other seats changed over every few stops, and the bus filled up. People who couldn't get a seat crowded together, trying to find something to hold on to. Their wet coats touched each other. At one of the stops the young priest from Jaffa who conducted the Mass in Polish got on. Emilia was surprised to see him outside the church. His presence on the bus were foreign, strange, as though he were not supposed to be there or were there only for her. And he looked completely different. His clerical collar peeked out under a blue sweater and a black windbreaker, and on his shoulder he carried a leather satchel, like a student.

The priest did not notice Emilia because she was hidden behind a huddle of passengers. She could only see him when one of the passengers moved or got off and the crowd broke up. His face, which appeared and disappeared intermittently in her line of sight, excited Emilia. Since no one offered him a seat, she got up, leaving her plastic bag on the bench, and made her way towards him. She did not introduce herself when she asked, in English, if he would like to sit down. He gave her a surprised look, smiled and said he was getting off at the next stop.

She went back to her seat and got off a few stops later, on the corner of Bialik and Aba Hillel streets.

GIL WAS BUSY, AND she waited for him in an armchair in front of a secretary.

Two stout men who looked like twins left his office, but she kept waiting until the secretary told her she could go in and walked her to his office. The soft, white, doughy hand that Gil held out when she walked in reminded her of Nachum's hands, which she used to wash every morning and evening, and once every week or two she would clip his nails. His green eyes also resembled Nachum's, but they did not look at her as directly as Nachum used to when he woke up in a fright or when she washed his face.

Gil wore a suit and smelled of aftershave. At the beginning of the meeting he still looked busy or distracted. He told Emilia in Hebrew, 'My mother said you went to see her and that you'd like my advice.' Emilia understood what he said, but she answered in English. In fact, she didn't need anything from him now, because soon she would start a full-time job at the nursing home, but when he asked her in English, 'So how can I help you?' she lied and repeated the things that were correct when she'd told them to Esther: She works part-time, the pay is not enough, she wants to start cleaning homes or offices on her free days. She doesn't know if she should do it without permits or try to change her work permit, if that's even possible. Esther suggested she ask Gil, which was why she'd called. She felt bad about not telling

Gil the truth, but consoled herself with the knowledge that what she had told Esther was not a complete lie and it had been true when she'd called him.

All she knew about Gil at this point was that he was Nachum and Esther's youngest son. A few years younger than his two sisters and many years younger than his brother. Of the four, he was the one who visited Nachum and Esther the least, and not simply because he was busy and travelled overseas a lot – or so she understood from what Esther sometimes said. Esther had insinuated that he visited his in-laws much more often, because they were rich and gave Gil and his wife a lot of money. Emilia remembered hearing her tell Nachum that 'Gil knew who to marry in terms of money, but that hasn't helped him be happy in life.' Emilia did not see him often. Money matters and her salary were handled by their oldest son, Ze'ev.

His office was small and not very fancy. There was grey wall-to-wall carpeting, and the furniture was old. Not only his hands and the colour of his eyes reminded Emilia of his father, Nachum, but also something in the soft slowness of his movements.

The woman he had married was named Ruthi, and Emilia did not see her often either. They had two daughters, Hadass and Noa, who came to visit Nachum and Esther without him, alone or together. During the shiva Esther had brought out old photo albums, and on Saturday, when there were no visitors, she'd shown Emilia pictures of Gil as a boy and as a teenager.

When Gil asked her for her passport and the papers from the employment agency and looked through them, Emilia thought it was possible that the little room she'd slept in for two years used to be his childhood room.

Gil looked up from the documents at Emilia. He told her in English that this wasn't exactly his field now, but that he'd worked on these matters until a few years ago, with agencies and foreign workers. In his opinion it would be next to impossible to change her work permit, certainly unless there were a formal request from the agency that had brought her to Israel.

'Would you like me to contact them and ask them to submit a request?' he asked, and Emilia quickly said no.

'Then, as an attorney, I cannot recommend that you work without the correct permits.' After a pause, he added, 'But it might be the easiest way. That's what everyone does. Including Israelis. But give me a few days to make a couple of enquiries and get back to you, okay?'

Emilia nodded but did not leave yet. It was important that he understand that she did not want him to get in touch with the agency, and he said he understood. He asked how to pronounce her last name and when she repeated it twice, *Nodyeves*, because Gil had trouble pronouncing it, she thought about how she hadn't said her last name for a long time, as if the only name she had left was Emilia – *eh-mi-li-ya* – and that, too, was vanishing, because Adina did not call her by her name, as Nachum and Esther had. For a moment her name came back to her, thanks to Gil. When he asked if she had any relatives in Israel she said no, and Gil switched to Hebrew and asked, 'But in Latvia? Do you have family in Riga?' She shook her head. 'Not in Latvia either? No children in Latvia?'

She had no children. And now no parents either. She wanted to tell him that his father and mother were the last family she'd had, but that was not true because she also had her Aunt Stefka and her two cousins, both of whom had children. Then Gil mentioned Nachum. He said, 'I know how attached Dad was to you. Have you been a caregiver for a long time? Before you came to Israel were you also a caregiver?' Emilia said no, and she told him that in Riga she'd worked at a hoomeware shop. She took her black purse out of the plastic bag, but Gil motioned for her to put it back. He said, 'You don't have to pay me, absolutely not. There's nothing to pay for yet. I'll let you know if there is. And I'll try to do what I can to help.'

THAT EVENING EMILIA WALKED all the way to Jaffa. The Polish Mass started at six o'clock, and she got there early and sat for a while in the square outside the church, by the sea.

She thought about the priest on the bus, earlier that morning. About how she might not be able to go to Mass on Sundays once she worked full-time and lived in the nursing home. The sight of the young priest among the passengers on the bus was a sign that she had to speak with him, and she decided to do it that day.

By now she knew exactly when all the worshippers would get up from their wooden pews and when they would kneel. She thought about the fold-out couch in the tiny living room in Adina's flat and about the old sheets she would sleep on. The priest's voice fell from the church ceiling and propelled her thoughts to other things, like

Nachum's hands, which were almost the only part of his body that had no signs of impending death or old age. She thought about how similar they were to the soft hand Gil had held out that morning. She thought about how the hands of the Son of God in the statue behind the priest were not injured, unlike the rest of his body. The hands of the marble Son of God were white and slender and the fingers were long and clean, with no signs of having been stabbed by nails. For a moment Nachum appeared before her again, but this time only in her memory. They were in the bathroom, at the sink. He sat in his wheelchair and she stood beside him, holding his hands, placing them above the sink and bathing them in water and soap. Nachum, perhaps because the mirror was too high and he could not look into his own face, looked at hers. She also thought about her mother, who fell ill when Emilia was a young girl who did not know how to be near death without being frightened by it, and about her father, who died suddenly many years later, from a heart attack, without Emilia having time to look after him.

The priest said nothing about their encounter that morning on the bus and neither did she. She wondered if it had really been him. She asked him in English if she could speak with him, and the priest asked her to wait while he said goodbye to the congregants. Then he beckoned for her to follow him, and they went to the priests' room down the hallway, behind the prayer hall.

It was a large, hot room. They sat on wooden chairs at a long table covered with a red tablecloth. The young priest asked Emilia if she wanted a drink of water and she said yes. How did he know she was so thirsty?

As she'd feared, Emilia had trouble talking when she sat facing him. She could not find the right words.

From up close he looked so young, even younger than she'd thought. Younger than the age her son or daughter would be today if she hadn't miscarried. His eyes were green, too, like Nachum's and his son Gil's. The priest could tell she was having trouble starting and he tried to help, asking her name and where she was from and how long she'd been in Israel. He asked if she'd been coming to church since she'd moved here, and she shook her head and said only in the past few weeks. When he asked why now, if something had happened in her life that had made her start coming, she became confused and said she didn't know. The priest smiled and said, 'Perhaps my question is wrong, actually. You don't need a reason to start going to church.'

He poured more water from a glass carafe into her empty glass, and told her that he'd been in Israel only for a few weeks. His name was Tadeusz. He was born in a little town near Poznan, in Poland, and for the past two years he'd lived and worked in Sheffield in England. He was still getting used to life in Israel. The things he said really did help Emilia. She managed to ask Tadeusz, 'Did you request to come here?' He said no, and when she did not say anything, he added, 'We do not request. Not usually. We can try, but we almost always go wherever we are sent. Did you want to come here?'

Emilia shook her head and put her glass down on the table and suddenly felt able to talk. She told him about Nachum, about how before she came here she didn't know who she was going to care for, but the moment she'd seen him she'd felt there was a reason she'd been sent to care for him, perhaps to make amends for not having cared for her mother when she'd been ill many years ago, or for her father. She said that now, when she was no longer caring for Nachum, she didn't know if she should stay in Israel or go back to Riga. She was searching for the reason she was here but had not found it yet. Caring for Adina could not be the reason, but she felt that the fact that she was here was no coincidence. Then she plucked up the courage to ask the question she'd wanted to ask the priest since she'd first entered the church: 'How do we know if we're on path He intends for us, or if we should go different way? If we're wrong and should change direction?'

When Tadeusz smiled at her, Emilia was certain he was the man she'd seen that morning on the bus. It was the same generous smile he'd given her when she'd offered her seat. His face was as soft as a child's and his hair smooth and fair, and he ran his hand through it while he talked. He said, 'We do not know, Emilia. Or at least most of the time we don't, I think. Most of the time we don't know, and only sometimes there are brief moments of knowing inside us, and we try to follow them. I don't know you well enough yet, but I think you are walking on the path He has intended for us, because I believe that He always guides us to help others – and that is exactly what you are doing.'

ON THE WAY HOME Emilia stops at the homeware shop on Balfour Street. The shopkeeper recognizes her by now. She doesn't know that her name is Emilia Nodyeves, nor how old she is or what she does in her life, and that she should not be spending so much money at the shop. But she does know the thin older lady whose hair is short and fair and who almost always wears baggy grey jeans and a grey short-sleeved T-shirt, even on cold days, and large sunglasses with red frames, and who spends a long time in the shop. And even though there is no point in Emilia buying anything for the flat she is soon leaving, she buys a set of decorative coasters and a little copper bell with a string that can be hung from a window frame.

On her remaining evenings in the flat she makes sweet tea and copies into her notebook Hebrew words and sentences she gathers from newspapers or brochures she finds in the nursing home lobby. She keeps drawing the name *Emilia* in Hebrew, and also writes *Jaffa* and *Tadeusz* and *St Peter Simon Cephas*.

Nachum sometimes appears in her room and sits next to her while she draws the characters in pencil, and she does not dare look at him. His skin is slowly disappearing, his eyes are growing darker. She wants to ask Tadeusz about the world after this world, about the place where her mother and father and Nachum went, but for now she prefers not to because she is afraid of alarming him. And she knows she will not tell him about seeing Nachum anyway.

She sets the alarm clock to wake her early in the mornings, so that she can prolong her time alone. She drinks her coffee in the winter light at the open window.

5

THE FIRST OF MARCH arrives. Emilia packs her belongings in two suitcases again. She has new homeware that she wraps in newspaper and buries among her clothes. In the nursing home she transfers them to a cardboard box that she is given by a Moldovan kitchen worker, which she places on the floor in the corner of Adina's balcony, under a plastic chair, where it is protected from the rain that will soon stop.

Adina wakes up frequently at night, crying and yelling. Emilia gets up from her sofa bed and goes to her, and to her surprise she is able to calm her. She strokes Adina's withered arm and thinning hair until she falls asleep. Those are the good moments. In the daytime Adina grumbles and curses, and even tries to hit Emilia when she helps her get dressed. Her health seems to be declining, and sometimes she does not remember who Emilia is.

NOW EMILIA HAS TWO homes to miss: the little room at Esther and Nachum's, which is slowly fading from her memory, and the flat that was hers for several weeks in Bat Yam, with the traffic and the neighbours' voices coming through the window. In the nursing home she has neither a room nor a bed. Every evening she folds out the sofa in the living room, takes a sheet, blanket and pillow from the linen box underneath and makes her bed for the night. Every morning she removes the linens, puts them back in the box and folds up the bed.

What is especially difficult for her is that she has no quiet moments. And without that quiet she cannot hear anything, she cannot understand where He is guiding her, and she gets lost. She gets up early, but the minute she turns on the tap to wash her face, Adina wakes up. In the evenings she can hear her breathing heavily in the bedroom. Her restlessness gets worse. Even when she tries to escape, she cannot. The other caregivers have a lively social life in the evenings, and when Emilia leaves Adina's room she meets people in the hallways and lifts, and groups of caregivers sitting in the courtyard ask her to join them. The second thing she suffers from is the smell. The smell of the nursing home is different from the smell of old age in her father's house or at Nachum and Esther's. It is now the smell that engulfs her life, and it makes it difficult for her to breathe.

Only on Sundays does Emilia remember that she is still searching. Hava begrudgingly gives her four free hours, and she walks to the Jaffa port, arriving long before Mass, and waits for Tadeusz on the front pew. When he walks into the prayer hall he sees Emilia first, and after prayers he invites her to the priests' room. He can tell that she is increasingly distraught, but when he asks if she's eating she says yes. She does not hide her anguish, but in their conversations she gives it different names. She asks him about the searching, about the lack of understanding, and Tadeusz says that in life there are misunderstood periods, weeks or months or even years when there is seemingly nothing but meaningless suffering, and that often it turns out later that these were in fact periods or preparation, of ripening.

Emilia says she knows that, but when she is in the nursing home she finds it impossible to believe. Tadeusz explains that precisely because that is where it's most difficult for her, that is where she must be for now. He reminds her of the forty days when the Son of God was in the desert without bread, being tested by Satan, and after that He began to spread the revelation. To lift her spirits, Tadeusz asks Emilia which language she prefers to read in, and promises to bring her a copy of the New Testament. But he also wonders if she should ask the agency about a different job and whether she is in touch with anyone from her family. He is so young, and when she looks at his smooth face she frequently thinks that he could have been her son, if she had had a son. The skin on his face is golden, as though anointed with olive oil. Despite his youth he is full of quiet confidence when he speaks, and there is something reassuring in his eyes. He tells her, 'Each of us is in this place for a purpose. You knew that before you met me, and that is why you came and asked to talk to me. Not so that I could help you find the purpose, but so that I could accompany you on the road you are taking towards it. And if you are patient and brave, I know you will find it.'

SHE DOES NOT THINK about her meeting with Gil until he calls her, and she even sees Nachum less now, because she is always at the home with Adina and Nachum is usually revealed to her only when she is alone.

Gil phones on a Tuesday evening, just after nine. A strange time. Adina is asleep and Emilia is just getting her bed ready. She answers in a whisper and takes the phone out to the hallway.

Gil asks how she is and apologizes for taking so long to get back to her. He also apologizes for not having good news. At first Emilia does not remember what he's talking about. Her life has changed so much since she moved into the home that her previous life has been erased. Gil says he hasn't given up completely but it doesn't seem that he'll be able to change her work permit without a formal request from the agency. If Emilia wants to take on extra work, she will have to do it without a permit. She doesn't tell him that there's no need any more – how can she tell him when he's made such an effort for her? She even asks how much she owes him and hopes she can get hold of the sum.

He says there's no need to pay because he was unsuccessful.

After a pause he says that even though there is still a small chance he'll manage to change the permit, he wants to give her back the documents she left with him because she probably needs them. She suggests coming to his office when she has a morning off, but he says he's in Bat Yam and can drop them off at her flat. She continues to lie, perhaps so that he doesn't find out she's already got a full-time job and his efforts were wasted, or perhaps for a different reason. She doesn't tell him that she left her flat and moved into the home. When he asks if she can come down and meet him outside so he doesn't have to find parking, she says yes, but that she isn't at home now and can only get there in half an hour.

It is a surprising event, not yet understood, in a routine of days and nights that contain so few unexpected occurrences.

Emilia puts a white sweater on over her grey T-shirt because the evenings are cool. A moment before she leaves the room, Adina wakes up and calls her name, but Emilia manages to get her back to sleep quickly. She takes the route she used in the weeks when she walked from the nursing home to the flat. The grocery where she bought fruits and vegetables and bottled water is open and the shopkeeper is smoking a cigarette on the pavement outside, but the homeware shop is closed. The kitchen window where Emilia liked to sit is shuttered and the flat is dark, probably because it hasn't been let, but the flat upstairs is lit and familiar sounds emerge from it. Emilia remembers. The husband and his wife are still fighting. All that was only a short while ago, but it has drowned in the depths of her memory during her distressing days at the nursing home.

Her phone rings, and at the same moment a big car pulls up.

Emilia steps on to the street and goes over to the car window and Gil holds out his soft hand. The documents are on a briefcase sitting on the passenger seat. He apologizes again for not being able to get her permit and reiterates that he hasn't given up. He asks if Emilia has spoken to his mother recently. Emilia feels guilty for not talking to Esther and asks Gil how she is. He starts telling her that she's having a rough time, but then he stops because his car is in the middle of the street. He asks if Emilia wants to get a cup of coffee and she gets into the car and sits down next to him in the front seat, which he clears of papers and the briefcase.

Emilia has to get back to the home because she mustn't leave Adina alone for too long.

Gil leans over and puts his hand under her feet to show her how to move the seat back. He asks if she knows any cafés nearby, but she hasn't been to a café since she came to Israel. During the short drive, Gil continues to tell her about Esther, who rarely leaves the house and had a bad case of flu that turned into pneumonia, and Emilia is sure he's going to ask her to leave her job and come to care for his mother.

No one else is in the café by the boardwalk. Emilia asks the waitress for a coffee and remembers the morning when she took the bus to Gil's office in Ramat Gan and saw Tadeusz. She tries not to let the happiness inside her break free too soon but it's not easy. Gil looks at her with Nachum's eyes. His slow movements and the way he sits on his chair also belong to his father, and Emilia is certain he's going to ask her if she can take care of Esther – there could be no other reason for them sitting there. In her imagination she goes back to the little room and puts her suitcase under the narrow bed, but a moment later she discovers that the conversation has a different purpose.

When Emilia asks Gil how his wife and daughters are, he says nothing. Perhaps he's debating what he might say to this older woman who was once his father's caregiver but with whom he'd barely exchanged more than a few words before tonight. Then, as if having decided that he can talk to her, he starts by saying that he is also going through a difficult time. He asks Emilia not to tell Esther if she sees her, and explains that he and his wife are getting divorced.

It was planned long ago but postponed because of Nachum's illness and then his death. Now they've decided there's no point in waiting. 'I don't know if you've ever been married,' he says, 'but if so, I'm sure you understand. We're at a point where it can't go on any longer.' Gil says he's rented a flat near their house, and he has to get it ready for him and his daughters, who will split their weeks between the two homes. When he asks Emilia if she knows anyone who could deep-clean the rental flat and help him get it set up, she offers herself because she is sure that is what he wants, and is surprised when at first he says that's not what he meant.

Emilia forces herself not to be disappointed. She insists that she'll be happy to clean his flat but she can only do it on Sundays. If Hava agrees to let her leave the home earlier, she'll have time to work for Gil before church.

'What's important is that you not tell Mum, if you talk to her, because it's the last thing she needs to hear. We don't want to upset her, she's having a hard time as it is,' he adds.

Emilia tells Gil she has to leave, still without disclosing that she must get back to the nursing home. They drive there in his car, he stops and lets her off in front of the building on Balfour Street, and Emilia walks in and waits for Gil to drive away before she goes back on to the dark street and walks to the home.

On the way she gets a first text message from him. He writes, in English:

> Thank you for everything, Emilia. I'm glad we met. And on second thoughts, can you come on Sunday?

6

SUNDAY, SHORTLY BEFORE NOON, first visit to Gil's flat.

Emilia waits for him on Balfour Street, in front of the building where he thinks she lives. The idea of having to clean his place did not make her happy when she woke up, and the disappointment that he hadn't asked her to care for Esther, as she'd believed he would, still stung. But when he picks her up he is smiling and pleasant, says he's pleased to see her and asks how she is. That is a big change after a gloomy morning with Adina and Hava, who came to take over from Emilia and made sure to let her know that she was not happy about giving Emilia every Sunday off. This is the second time Emilia has been in Gil's car, and the proximity to him in the closed space takes her back to Nachum.

Gil says he visited Esther over the weekend and told her he'd seen Emilia. Esther sent warm regards and kisses. She is happy they are in touch. He tells her that he encouraged his mother to go out and she promised to take up swimming again. He says his mother misses Emilia, and wonders if she doesn't miss the neighbourhood where she lived for two years. Emilia says she does. He did not tell Esther anything about the flat Emilia is going to help clean, because she doesn't know about the divorce and he isn't planning to tell her for now. He doesn't ask Emilia to visit or phone Esther. When he stops the car, Emilia unbuckles her seatbelt because she thinks they've arrived, but Gil says, 'Not yet. Hold on, I have to buy a few things for you. I'll be right back.' In the bag he holds when he gets back into the car there are bottles of floor and bathroom cleaner, rags, rubber gloves, and ropes that he will ask Emilia to attach to two rusty iron rods sticking out of the exterior wall under the bathroom window, to use for hanging laundry. As they drive he says, 'I feel bad that you're ending up doing this. Are you sure this is how you want to spend your day off?' But Emilia does not regret it, and when they walk into his flat for the first time, she knows she was not wrong.

SHE LIKES IT FROM the first moment.

Gil opens the door, turns on the living-room light and says, in Hebrew, 'So this is it.' As he walks her around the rooms, he says no one has lived there for a few months and he only started sleeping there less than two weeks ago. He still needs to get rid of some things the previous tenants left. Apart from superficially cleaning the toilet and bathroom and his bedroom, he hasn't had time to do much because of his long hours at the office and an overseas trip, and also because he doesn't know how to turn someone else's flat into a home. There are two small bedrooms, each with a matching kid's bed, desk and double-door wardrobe, and Gil says they will be Noa and Hadass's rooms when they come to stay, three times a week. The master bedroom does look slept in – the large bed is covered with a blue sheet and a blanket, and there are three pillows scattered on it – and in the living room are a couch, a coffee table and a television on the wall. The walls in all the rooms are bare.

'It doesn't look like home yet, but it could, don't you think?' he says when they go back to the living room. Then he disappears into one of the rooms and Emilia is left alone. He returns with a bucket and mop and asks Emilia how long she thinks she'll need.

AFTER HE LEAVES, EMILIA walks around, opening the blinds and windows to let in some air and light. The air is cool and warm at the same time and the light is bright. Spring sunshine. She is alone after so long.

She takes off her jeans and T-shirt in the bathroom and puts on sweatpants and a red sweatshirt that she brought in a plastic bag. The last time she wore those clothes was when she cleaned the one-room flat in Bat Yam and set it up, and its smell is still on the clothes. Gil's place floods her with other memories too. It reminds her of her parents' home after she removed their belongings to get it ready for the music teacher who rented it after her father died. The two narrow bedrooms with kid's beds remind Emilia of her own room at Nachum's, and also of her childhood room, even though that room did not have a window. She thinks about Noa and Hadass, who will come to stay here, about how they will have rooms in two different homes, and she tries to imagine what the rooms will look like once they fill them with their stuff and hang pictures and mirrors. It's been so long since she's seen a young girl's room. For so long she has spent time only in the rooms of people with death crawling inside them, or in empty rooms that contain no life.

Even though Gil did not ask her to, she opens the wardrobes in the girls' rooms and finds them empty. She cleans them thoroughly, first with a duster and then with a cloth that she dips and wrings out in a yellow bowl of water she found in a utility cupboard on the balcony. She spends the most time on the girls' rooms, as if they were going to be hers. Then she moves to the master bedroom, shakes out the blanket and pillows and puts them to air on the windowsill, which looks out on to a little courtyard where Emilia thinks she sees, for the first time that day, just for an instant, Nachum, sitting under the shade of a tree, the way they used to sit together when he was alive. The old wardrobe that covers an entire wall reminds her of the one in her parents' bedroom because of the strong smell of mothballs when she opens it, and because of the shelves made of thin, light wood. A few shirts are folded on them, two pairs of trousers hang, and in one drawer there are a few pairs of underwear and socks. In the bottom drawer, meant for shoes, Emilia finds a plastic bag with hundreds of foreign-currency coins, two pens, some old-looking notebooks and a file, and three newspapers, two in Hebrew and one in a different language. She doesn't know if these things belong to Gil or if they were forgotten by the previous tenants. When she takes them out of the drawer to dust it, she finds that in the three newspapers there is a photograph of the same woman, roughly her age or a little younger, and she places them with the pens and notebooks and the bag of coins on the floor next to the bedroom door, ready to be thrown out if they turn out not to be Gil's.

Her phone beeps from the kitchen, and she finds a message from Gil: 'If you want me to pick you up earlier, let me know. I'm nearby.' Then she thinks she hears the front door shut and she goes to the living room, but no one has come in, and she realizes it must have been the door in another flat. Since evening is near and the sky is overcast and it might rain, she shuts the blinds and windows when she finishes washing all the floors, towards half past four. She only leaves the window in Gil's room slightly open, to let in the fading light that filters through the blinds and falls on the bed.

GIL IS SURPRISED AND delighted to find the flat so clean – Emilia can see that when he gets back.

He goes into the girls' rooms and his own bedroom and is impressed by the newly shiny floor and furnishings. When he sees the pile of rubbish Emilia left by the door, and next to it the things she took out of the drawers in his room, his eyes darken for a moment, and she thinks she should not have opened the wardrobes and drawers. She explains that she wasn't sure if they were his or the previous tenants', and he says they belong to the old tenants. But he puts them back in his room and explains that he'll sort them out later and throw away what needs to be thrown away.

He drives Emilia to Jaffa.

On the way he asks if she had time to get lunch, and when she says no, he suggests they stop at a restaurant, but Emilia cannot be late. Gil says next time he can pick her up earlier, and that is the first time he hints that he would like her to come again.

There is an awkward moment when he pulls up by a square full of tourists and asks how much he owes her. Emilia doesn't know. He says, 'Fifty shekels an hour is good, right? I'll pay you for five hours. And before next time, why don't you ask around what the going rate is? I can find out too.' He hands her the money in cash, three bills of a hundred, and adds, 'Mostly, I hope you don't regret coming.' Emilia quickly puts the cash in her pocket, without counting it or giving him change, as if it were money she did not deserve or would not want anyone to see her taking. After Mass she puts all the bills Gil gave her, still clumped together from the dampness in her pocket, into the donation basket that is passed around, and she thinks she sees Tadeusz looking at her just when she does that. He doesn't say anything about it when they sit facing each other in the priests' room afterwards, and Tadeusz asks how she is and how her week has been. She doesn't say anything either, for now, about her feeling that today might have been the day when He brought her to the place she was supposed to reach, that perhaps the waiting and searching will soon be over. But she does pluck up the courage to tell Tadeusz about seeing Nachum, and the young priest looks at her understandingly.

'You see him because you miss him, isn't that so? And probably other people too,' he says.

'Yes. But I also see him because it is sign, because he wants to tell me something.' Then, alarmed by her own candidness, she asks him, 'Don't you think that's possible? That he really was there?'

Tadeusz says they can talk about the world that is not this world, but not today because it's a long conversation, which they both have to prepare for. He asks if the situation at the nursing home has improved and, for no reason, she says yes. Still, when she goes back to Adina she does feel more protected, as if the hours she spent working at Gil's have clarified something significant about her life or restored a part of herself. She can more easily tolerate Hava's furious looks for getting back late and another night on the sofa bed. Adina wakes up shouting in the middle of the night, and Emilia stays with her for a long time until she calms down, warming the old lady's fingers with her hands.

Before the next time she goes to Gil's flat, she pulls out the cardboard box she'd stored on the balcony, removes the embroidered tablecloth and brings it with her to spread on the table in his dining area.

7

All at once spring arrives. The forty days of Lent are coming to an end. The mornings are cool but the afternoon sun floods Adina's room, and when Emilia hangs the linens out to air on the balcony, she sees the first bathers on the beach.

The Mass also changes, becoming more severe. Longer. The fate of the Son of God is more present in the prayer hall and in the worshippers' hearts. Soon it will be the time of the crucifixion, the torments, the temporary death and the resurrection. Tadeusz urges Emilia to go to confession before Holy Week so that she can receive Communion, but Emilia refuses because there are things she cannot confess. She merely insinuates to Tadeusz that she has found the place and the road, and that her search might be over.

*

GIL PICKS HER UP every Sunday before noon from Balfour Street and takes her to the flat. On the way he tells her about his mother and his divorce. He says Esther's condition is not improving, her depression is affecting her health and she will soon need full-time care. She rarely leaves home, because of her grief over Nachum's death and her loneliness, and does not even do simple grocery shopping. Emilia's heart goes out to Esther, but she does not dare tell Gil that she wants to care for her, because she still hopes the offer will come from him. Esther's health is preventing Gil from telling her about his separation, which is now official. The divorce papers are signed and the property divided. Since his wife makes a lot less than he does, he gave her most of the assets and will also pay significant alimony so that she can maintain a respectable lifestyle. Custody arrangements for Noa and Hadass are also finalized, and they are supposed to start staying with him soon, when they feel ready and his home is set up for them. For now he sleeps alone in the big, empty flat.

Emilia doesn't talk much in these conversations. She listens to him. She hears the language of things.

Gil explains that the girls need time, they are finding it harder to accept the divorce than he and his wife are, but they came over one day to see the flat and they liked it. 'It'll be good for them, too, eventually,' he says.

FROM THE MOMENT GIL moves in, the flat becomes filled with life, even though he has very few belongings. A carton of milk, a tub of cream cheese and an open bottle of wine appear in the clean refrigerator. In the bathroom there is shampoo, shower gel, shaving cream and a new razor.

Emilia unpacks the cardboard box she stored over winter under the chair on Adina's balcony. She puts the basket meant for baked goods or fruit on Gil's dining table, and hangs the copper bell from the bedroom window that overlooks the garden with two trees where she saw Nachum on her first visit. When Gil notices Emilia's additions, he thanks her and wants to pay her back, but she refuses. She explains that she bought them for herself and has no need for them because she will probably have to leave her flat soon and move in with the lady she cares for at the nursing home.

Gil asks if she wouldn't rather stay in her own place, and she says of course she would, but she may not have a choice. He enquires about her financial situation and asks if she needs more money. He still does not raise the possibility of her going back to live with Esther or moving into his flat, but he does tell Emilia that if she needs anything, she should not hesitate to ask: 'Do you need to send money to anyone at home?' She says no.

'But if you do, you'll ask me, right? I would be really happy to help you, Emilia.'

Sometimes he stays in the flat while Emilia works. Other times he goes to his office for an urgent meeting and comes back early with lunch for them both in plastic takeaway containers. Schnitzel with roast potatoes and green beans, or Thai food, which Emilia finds too spicy. Gil sets the table while Emilia changes from her work clothes into a clean outfit, blue jeans and a white shirt she bought recently in Jaffa.

He watches Emilia. At the nursing home she still puts nothing in her mouth except vegetables and the occasional apple, but at his place she eats, albeit slowly, aware of the way her mouth is moving, because he watches her. During one meal he tells her he's started going to the gym and riding a bike. He is also coming to life, like the flat. From one conversation to the next he talks more about Nachum's death and the way it changed him. Emilia listens thirstily, not only because his words arouse memories of Nachum but because she senses he is talking about her, too, and about her father's sudden death, not only about himself.

He offers Emilia a glass of white wine with her meal, and on the second time of asking she agrees. She has finished cleaning. Since she hasn't had any alcohol for a long time, the wine affects her quickly. A warmth spreads through her body and she feels her bare feet on the cool floor. She had never been fond of wine. And their conversation is confusing. Gil looks at Emilia's neck and her flushed cheeks and says quietly that she doesn't talk much. He asks why. He asks whether she feels lonely in Israel and if she's homesick, and she says that when she was with Nachum and Esther she did not feel alone, but now she does.

'Where do you call home? Is your home here now, or there?' he asks, and she does not answer. When he asks if she's ever been married, she turns red and takes another sip of wine and then says no, without confessing to what was once almost a wedding, many years ago, but ended with a broken heart and a stillborn foetus at seven and a half months.

After they finish eating, Gil washes the dishes and Emilia clears the table. The flat is painted in the setting sun's light that comes in through the blinds and gives off a lemony-clean scent.

Gil is grateful to Emilia. He says that without her he couldn't have made a home for Noa and Hadass, and he feels that she's helping him start his new life. More and more he understands why Nachum was so attached to her, he says, and that makes Emilia feel guilty for hiding the fact that she doesn't have her own place and is staying with Adina in the nursing home.

She says he doesn't have to thank her. She believes that everything happens for a reason. Gil thinks so too. Her face responds to his smile. When his fingers move close to her for the first time, she shuts her eyes and struggles to think about Nachum's hands. She used to hold them in a basin with hot water and some baby oil to soften the skin. She tended patiently to his nails.

He runs his fingertips over her narrow forehead and her cheeks and chin, then moves down to her neck, and Emilia shuts her eyes harder, but she still knows Nachum is watching them with his torn black eyes because she saw him earlier in the living room. She wants Gil to stop because his father is watching, but she will not tell him that. Nachum is there almost all the time now, with his mouth open, looking grey. She thinks about Tadeusz's fingers, too, those olive-oil fingers when he holds the carafe and fills her empty glass with water, and about the long, white marble fingers of the sculpted Son of God that she looks at during Mass.

Gil's fingers are soft and slow over her clothes and under them.

Lingering on every spot on her skin, sharpening it with their touch. Emilia wants to think about other things when his fingers climb up her neck and when she smells his breath close to her face for the first time. She must visit Esther and she must go back to Adina at the nursing home, she thinks, and out of those two senses of obligation her father also appears behind her closed eyes, as if she needs to take care of him, too, and may be given the opportunity to.

WHEN SHE STEPS OUT of Gil's car outside the church he says, 'See you next Sunday?' But he starts sending her text messages in the middle of the week. Usually late at night, at nine or half past nine, after Adina goes to sleep. He writes in Hebrew: 'Can you meet, Emilia? I miss your smell and your body.' Emilia sometimes answers him in Hebrew: 'I can come in half hour,' because she needs time to get dressed and put on make-up and get to Balfour Street.

Emilia's time is short.

She has to make sure Adina is sleeping deeply enough for her to shower off the smell of the home. She opens Adina's jewellery box, which is buried deep in her wardrobe and locked with a key that she hides in her bedside-table drawer, and she borrows a pair of earrings and a very thin gold chain with no pendant. She hopes the front-desk receptionist thinks she's going outside to talk with other caregivers in the garden or to sit on the boardwalk, and that none of them sees her when she leaves the building and walks towards Balfour Street, and especially not when she comes back an hour or two later. She hopes Adina doesn't wake up and call her name while she's gone.

They sit at the café where they went the first time, and sometimes they sit in Gil's car. In the dark, in an empty car park by the beach.

He is capable of touching her lustfully, but can also touch slowly, moving back to see her face as he walks his soft fingers along her body, from her forehead to her thighs, over her clothes.

Not a single car enters the car park, and when Gil turns off the headlights the darkness around them is complete.

Emilia explains that she must get home because the next day she has to be at Adina's early, and Gil says, 'Just a few more minutes. It's so quiet here.' He opens a window to listen to the sea and then shuts it because the wind is cold.

'I feel so good with you, Emilia. Do you feel that way too? That this is the beginning of the new life I told you about? I want to help you, too, and protect you, so you'll be safe and feel that you have a home, do you understand what I mean? You deserve that, because of what you give me. Do you feel that I'm taking care of you and that you can be safe with me?'

8

WHEN EMILIA SOMETIMES WONDERS what she means to Gil, what she gives him or what he takes from her, she thinks her role is to help him set up a home and begin a new life after Nachum's death and the divorce. She believes that is the reason for her seeing Nachum in the flat, that he is trying to signal to her that she has reached the right place. At other times, especially when she tidies Gil's bedroom, she imagines herself waking up in the morning opposite the window with the trees and the copper bell, but she feels embarrassed by this imaginary picture, and she shoos it away from her thoughts. It is not herself that she should be thinking of. But Gil also seems guilt-ridden over what is happening between them. He asks her over and over again if it's okay. He says he will stop if he's doing something he should not do. He apologizes but then touches her face again. He didn't know this was what would happen between them. He tells Emilia again that he wants her to feel safe, to feel that she has a place that is like home, and that he wants to take care of her and does not want to hurt her. Emilia remembers the days when she was looking for work and a bed after Nachum's death and the hours she spent in the rented flat waiting for a sign. The despair. The car traffic on the street and the neighbours' voices coming through the window and then the move to the nursing home, with the three shelves Hava allotted her in Adina's wardrobe and the sofa she still folds out every night and covers with old sheets. She was waiting for Him to show her the way, and He led her to Gil, but she still does not know if this is only a station on the road she must take. So she never sends Gil messages or calls him on her own initiative – she lets him call and arrange things, and if he doesn't, she doesn't even wait.

In the evenings, after Adina falls asleep, Emilia keeps learning Hebrew from the notebook Nachum made her, because she feels that it's becoming more and more important that she know his language. And this time it is different, as if the time is right for Hebrew or as if Nachum's presence helps her, and thanks to him, the shapes become clearer and the words more familiar. She manages to read parts of signs in Hebrew at the nursing home, or when she takes the bus and Nachum is next to her, or in the homeware shop. If she comes across a word she doesn't know, she draws its shape in the notebook and sometimes asks Adina or Gil or one of the other caregivers what it means. Every evening she copies at least one complete Hebrew sentence into the notebook, from newspapers or brochures she finds in the lobby, or from the church leaflet, which is now always in her plastic bag. She draws slowly, in block letters: 'In Jaffa there was a student named Tabitha, meaning Tsivia, and she did many good deeds and acts of charity.' A childhood scene of her drawing letters with her father in a blue notebook at the dining table comes to life in her memory for a moment, then quickly fades, as if it had never existed. She also reads the messages Gil sends her in Hebrew and even manages to answer him every so often with brief messages in Hebrew letters.

He writes: 'I think about you a lot, Emilia.'

Or: 'I saw a shirt I want to buy you. Do you like blue?'

And then: 'I'm sorry I disappeared, Emilia. Can you meet me this evening, late, if possible?'

ADINA SENSES THAT SOMETHING is happening to Emilia, and so does Hava. When she comes to take over from Emilia on Sundays she asks where she's going and why she's wearing different clothes. She also interrogates Emilia about whether she ever goes out in the evening and leaves Adina alone, and Emilia says hardly ever, sometimes just for a few minutes to get some fresh air and chat with the other caregivers in the garden. She thinks the best thing that could happen to her now might be for Hava to catch her going out and fire her, so that she will have to look for a new bed and a new home.

She does tell Tadeusz a little more. He asks what Gil does and when he got divorced and how many children he has, and Emilia tells him about his grief for his father and his flat that is coming to life and the rooms for his two daughters and his generosity and all the money he gives his ex-wife. She does not disclose everything that happens between them, of course, but she does imply that she feels her meeting with Gil was no coincidence, that it is significant to her life. She remembers their first talk, when Tadeusz told her that we don't always know if we're on the path He meant for us, but that we have brief moments of knowing, and she feels that he was right. He also told her in that conversation that the way He guides us is always to help others, and that is also why she knows she is on the right path.

Tadeusz asks how Gil treats her and if he pays her for her work. He's noticed that Emilia leaves large sums of money in the donation basket, and he asks if she's sure she can afford it. She says she can but he asks her to put less money in the basket. She detects suspicion or disapproval in his look, and since it is a look that reminds her of Hava, she decides that from now on she will share less with Tadeusz. His tone in this conversation is also different. When he asks if Gil always stays in the flat while she is cleaning, Emilia decides to avoid talking to Tadeusz any more because she finds herself being defensive without wanting to be. She replies that Gil is not always there, that usually he's at work, even though the truth is that the only time he was not there while she worked was her last time.

IT HAPPENS TWO WEEKS before Easter. On Passion Sunday.

Gil texted her on Thursday to say he forgot to let her know

he'd be away for work on Sunday and she didn't need to come that week. But Emilia wrote to say she could take the bus. He replied, 'That would be great. And I have to see you later in the week. Can you?'

He left her a key in the fuse-box cupboard outside the flat, and because she knows the girls will be coming to stay for the first time the following week, she cleans especially thoroughly, particularly the kitchen and bathroom and the small bedrooms. The girls' wardrobes are still empty, but there is more life in the rest of the flat now. Emilia knows Gil is coming home the next day, and when she puts the colourful cushions she bought in the homeware shop on the couch she imagines the moment when he opens the door and turns on the living-room light. The wardrobe in his bedroom is not full yet either – he must have taken most of his clothes on the trip. In the bottom drawer she finds the files and notebooks and old newspapers with the picture of the woman she saw on her first visit. Instead of throwing them away he'd put them back, and Emilia understands from this that they belong to him and not to the previous tenants. She tries to read the headlines above the pictures in the old newspapers, but she stops at the third word because she does not understand it – 'Israeli Woman's Suicide' – and looks at the identical photographs. She wonders if she should borrow one of the papers and put it in her plastic bag so she can read more about the woman when she is back at the home. Then she lays the linens out to air on the windowsill she likes. The woman in the pictures intrigues her because she is connected to Gil, or rather because he is connected to her, and that is why she decides to keep reading about her. She knows it's not his ex-wife, because she saw her when they came to visit Nachum and Esther. The thought of Gil being connected to the woman in the pictures frightens Emilia for a moment, and she wants to know more about her, but she forbids herself to feel that way. She reminds herself that she is not there for herself but for him, and she thinks perhaps it is not a good idea for her to borrow the paper, but it does stay in her bag.

When the doorbell rings, Emilia is surprised because Gil is supposed to be away.

She stays in the bedroom, but when the bell rings again she goes to the door and looks through the peephole. She sees a young woman with short, dark hair. The woman must know that Emilia is there, because she rings yet again. When Emilia opens the door the woman apologizes for bothering her and says she lives in the flat across the hall and saw Emilia coming to clean, and she wants to know if she has time to clean another flat, today or any other day.

Emilia pretends not to understand Hebrew, and when the woman repeats herself in English, she answers, 'I don't know. Not today. Maybe next week.' The young woman is curious and Emilia thinks she's not only there about the cleaning but because she wants to see Gil's place. Since only a few minutes earlier she was looking at the face of the woman in the newspaper, she imagines for a moment that this neighbour could be the same woman, but it's not her. Before she leaves, the woman asks Emilia, 'What's your name?' and then she says, in English, 'I'm Yael. Nice to meet you. We'd be really happy if you could clean for us too. Can you tell me how much you charge an hour? Or is it based on the size of the flat?'

GIL GETS BACK THE next night and texts Emilia:

When can we meet?

THEY SIT IN HIS car by the boardwalk and he says nothing about the new cushions in the living room or how clean the flat is, but he gives Emilia some perfume he bought for her on his trip, wrapped in colourful paper with a blue ribbon. He asks her to open the package and drizzle some perfume on herself and he smells her neck, but she doesn't like the smell because it's too alcoholic. He also bought her a thin green silk scarf, which she likes much more than she shows him when she drapes it over her shoulders. He asks how Adina is and whether Emilia knows yet if she'll have to move in with her. He apologizes for being less delicate that evening. He tells Emilia, 'I thought about you a lot while I was away.'

Then he says he's had a great idea: he has another work trip over the Passover holiday, and he would like Emilia to go with him. No one has to know about it, neither his girls nor anyone else, and they can go for a really short trip, two or three days, even. He thought about it the whole time he was gone, and he knows where they should go.

Emilia is reluctant, and Gil asks, 'How long has it been since you went on holiday, Emilia? Not for two hours, I mean for a few days?'

She cannot remember how long it's been.

'And how long has it been since you went home?' he adds, and she looks at him uncomprehendingly.

Gil explains that his work trip is to Bucharest and he wants to take her to Riga afterwards. The thought of landing at Riga airport fills her with fear and excitement. Then he suggests, for the first time, that they go to Emilia's place, and he is disappointed when she refuses. She has no choice but to lie to him again, saying Adina is sick and she has to stay with her at the home tonight.

9

ONE NIGHT SOON AFTERWARDS, Emilia has a dream. She is cleaning her parents' place because they are about to come home after a long trip. She makes their bed, using sheets with a pattern of grey storks flying past clouds, which she remembers from her childhood. She dusts the familiar furniture and slowly draws a sign that says, in block letters, 'WELCOME HOME'. She makes dinner. The three of them are about to meet after a long time, and Emilia has to tell them that she is pregnant, and that this time there will not be a miscarriage. As she dreams she knows she can no longer get pregnant, but the logic of the dream cannot be controlled.

When the doorbell rings, Emilia hurries to open the door because she is sure her parents have arrived early, but instead there is a woman standing in the doorway who looks like Gil's neighbour, with short, dark hair, and also like the woman in the newspaper photographs, whose name is Orna. The neighbour asks if Emilia can help clean her flat, and Emilia isn't sure what to say. She knows her parents will be back any minute and that she won't have time to clean both places, but she finds it hard to say no because the woman's voice and eyes are genuinely pleading. 'Please,' she says to Emilia, 'I'll pay you however much you want. I need your help.' In the dream Nachum is also in her parents' home in Riga – Emilia knows this because she senses his presence in her sleep, and when she opens her eyes he is still there, next to the sofa bed in the nursing home.

When Emilia wakes up she immediately understands the reasons for the dream.

In the days after his return, Gil does not mention his work trip and his suggestion that Emilia join him, and she tells herself he must have changed his mind. But her imagination breaks through the walls of logic and gallops ahead, taking her back to Riga.

When they meet for the second time that week, on his initiative, Gil says nothing about it, and Emilia can't resist asking when he's going away. She tries to sound casual, as if she just wants to know when she should come and clean. He doesn't answer.

They go to their usual café and then to the dark car park by the boardwalk.

Gil apologizes and says he hasn't yet decided if he can extend his trip and take her with him. She can tell he's vacillating, perhaps even stepping back from the idea, and she's convinced it's because he's afraid she will think their relationship is too serious or because he's embarrassed to be seen with her, even though he says the uncertainty is because of work issues. Earlier that evening, Emilia had drizzled the perfume Gil bought her on her neck and wrists to make him happy, and the sharp scent had lingered in the lift at the nursing home for several minutes. She'd put on a skirt and a pair of pearl earrings borrowed from Adina's jewellery box. They do not talk about the trip any more, and Emilia tries not to look hurt or disappointed, but apparently she is unsuccessful, because a few minutes after Gil drops her off on Balfour Street, while she is walking back to the home, she gets several text messages from him: 'Would you go with me if I bought you a ticket?' 'Then let's do it.' And finally: 'Can you find out if you can get a few days off in the next two weeks?'

EMILIA ISN'T SURE THE trip is real, but she agrees and tries to find out if she can take time off. Hava is disinclined. 'Why do you need time off?' she asks, 'You only started working three months ago, didn't you? You're already tired out?' She says now is not a good time, and at such short notice it's complicated, because the days before Passover are busy and she and her family were planning to go away for the holiday.

'Where do you want to go, anyway?' she asks, and Emilia doesn't answer immediately. She doesn't tell Hava that in their last phone conversation Gil said he wanted to see where she was born and raised and asked if there was a particular place she would like to stay in, and if she wanted to let anyone know she was coming to visit.

Something in Hava's reaction seems unusual. Emilia can sense that it is creating a lot of tension between them. That weekend Hava visits them twice, at unexpected times and without notice. She still hasn't said yes or no, claiming she has to check with her husband, Meir. She asks Emilia again why she's giving her such short notice, why it's so urgent, how many days exactly she needs and if she couldn't put off the trip until summer.

Emilia could ask Gil to postpone the trip, but she doesn't want to because she is certain that by then he'll have changed his mind. In recent days she feels as if he's angry with her. His eyes are less soft and his fingers are cold and rigid. He looks suspicious.

On Good Friday, Hava pays an unexpected visit in the late evening, when Adina is asleep. She lets herself in with her key, without knocking first. Emilia is there because Gil didn't contact her that evening. She's in her pyjamas, and her hair is wet after a shower. She sits on a plastic chair on the balcony looking at the sea. Hava doesn't even bother explaining why she's come so late and doesn't look in on her mother. They talk about the trip, in whispers, on the balcony, and since Emilia doesn't want to lie but also cannot disclose the details, she says she was thinking of going to Riga to visit her family.

IN HER HEART EMILIA knows she is much more excited about the possibility of going home than she allows herself to acknowledge. And not only because of her dream. She thinks about how she will not have to care for Adina, and will be far away from the nursing home, and will sleep in a hotel on a made-up bed and not on the sofa in the tiny living room. She plans what clothes to pack and checks the weather forecast for Riga, even though Gil has not given her final confirmation and Hava hasn't authorized her leave. She has a grey coat with a wool lining that she hasn't worn even once in Israel.

She thinks back to her decision not to talk to Tadeusz any more because of his critical tone last time they met, but she can't keep her excitement to herself and so she looks forward to Sunday, when she can tell him. She knows how she will answer the questions Tadeusz asks and how she will explain to him why she wants to go, if he has reservations. He is the only person she can tell who she's going with because he knows about Gil and about Nachum, but she hasn't decided whether to tell him they're going away together or lie and say she's going alone. She is still afraid to believe that the trip is really happening, especially since Gil hasn't sent her a single message all weekend. When he doesn't turn up at Balfour Street to pick her up on Sunday, she is certain it's because he has changed his mind and doesn't know how to tell her.

Emilia goes into the homeware shop and waits for him there. She peeks through the display window to see if he's coming. The shopkeeper asks how she is, but this time Emilia doesn't buy anything, even though she has quite a bit of money in her purse. More than half an hour goes by. She leaves the shop and wonders if she should go back to the nursing home. She calls Gil but he doesn't answer, and she walks towards the centre of town. It's raining and she gets wet, because the morning was spring-like and she left without her denim jacket or an umbrella. For a few hours she feels as lost as she did when she'd just started working at the home, before she met

Gil, and she grows fearful. She doesn't want to go back to the room where Adina and Hava are waiting for her. She calls Gil again but he doesn't answer. She is sure now that he's angry with her, but she doesn't know what she did. Is it connected to the newspaper she took from his drawer? Did he notice before she could put it back? Since he'd kept three newspapers with her picture, Emilia realizes that the woman who committed suicide, Orna, was very dear to him, and sometimes she envies her.

When she gets to the church, more than half an hour before Mass, she is surprised by how many people are at the English-language Mass that is held before the Polish one, and also by the strong scent of incense and the great number of candles burning near the baptism font. It's Palm Sunday, which marks the beginning of Holy Week and Christ's final entry to Jerusalem, and so the church is more crowded than usual.

When the English Mass ends and the Filipino worshippers leave the hall, Emilia sits in her regular spot on the front pew, but the priest who comes in to hold Mass in Polish is not Tadeusz. It's a priest whom Emilia doesn't know, many years older than Tadeusz, taller, his skin very tanned and his hair turning white. He wears glasses. The priest tells the congregants that his name is Narcis, and his soft gaze meets Emilia's eyes, but she doesn't stay for the whole Mass. She gets up and goes into the priests' room behind the hall, but Tadeusz is not there either. When she asks where he is, she is told he's gone to spend Easter with his family in Poland. She feels almost hurt by him not telling her that he was leaving. Is he giving her a sign, even in his absence, or a confirmation that she should go if Gil wants her to? After all, he went home, too, just like she wishes to.

But the fear in those hours is stronger.

In the evening, when Emilia gets back, Hava is waiting for her. She tells Emilia that she talked to her husband, Meir, and it's all right for her to take a holiday, but she wants Emilia to give her the dates as soon as possible. Emilia thanks her. Although the trip now seems unreal, she asks how much time she can have and is surprised when Hava says she doesn't mind how many days she takes, as long as Hava knows when exactly the flight is so that she can prepare.

Emilia doesn't call Gil or send him a message, but he calls her that night. He apologizes for not coming to pick her up, explains that he was in unexpected meetings all day and wasn't able to answer her or call back because there was something wrong with his phone. His voice is cold but it still reassures her, and when he asks if Hava is letting her take time off she tells him that she is.

She still thinks she can hear doubt in his voice, or even regret, when he says, 'Really? She approved your holiday? Do you know when yet?' Then he says he'll call her back later that night.

When he phones after midnight, Emilia is going to suggest they forget about the trip, because she can sense that he doesn't want to do it. But then he sounds suddenly decisive, as if he's made up his mind, and he asks for her passport number and date of birth and full name as it appears on her passport.

And that night he books tickets.

*

OVER THE NEXT FEW days everything happens fast for Emilia, faster than she can digest, too fast to understand what is really going on.

She spends longer hours than usual with Adina, because Hava stops coming to see them; in fact, she disappears completely after Emilia lets her know when she's going away. Gil doesn't call or send messages all week either, as if he's changed his mind again, and when she calls him once he says he's extremely busy at work. Emilia misses Tadeusz very much. Since she has to talk to someone, she considers going to visit Esther, but she decides not to because she's afraid she won't be able to keep her relationship with Gil and their trip a secret, and Gil has repeatedly asked her not to say anything about the trip, especially not to his mother.

Instead she just calls Esther, but their conversation is short and disappointing. Full of silences.

Esther sounds confused, perhaps ill. She can't hear Emilia and hangs up on her. When Emilia calls back again, Esther can finally hear her name. Her voice is tired. She asks Emilia if she's still working at the nursing home, and Emilia says she is.

'Are you happy there now? Do they treat you well?'

She tells Emilia that her Hebrew sounds better, and Emilia answers in English that it's thanks to Nachum, thanks to his notebooks. When Esther says, 'Many things were thanks to Nachum. It's not easy for me to go on living without him,' Emilia asks herself again if she is the only one who sees him next to her all the time or if Esther does too.

With Adina, perhaps because she knows she'll soon get a break from caring for her, Emilia has some nice moments, like when they go out to the garden together to warm up in the afternoon sun, or at bedtime, when she holds Adina's fingers and waits for her to fall asleep.

When Gil texts her, he asks in Hebrew, 'Is everything ready, Emilia? Are you packed?' She isn't sure what he means and debates before writing back in Hebrew: 'I'm ready.'

Gil is supposed to fly to Romania on Sunday morning. He will have two full days of work in Bucharest, and Emilia will join him there on Tuesday evening. Her flight leaves Tel Aviv at 4 p.m. They will spend one day in Bucharest, then fly to Riga and stay through the weekend.

Emilia knows more or less where she will take him in Riga. The first place she wants to visit is her parents' home, and if the music teacher who took it over from them is still living there, she will ask if they can go inside.

They arrange for Gil to pick her up at Bucharest airport shortly before seven o'clock. If his meetings prevent him from getting there, Emilia will take a taxi to the hotel where he has booked a room, whose address Emilia copied down in her notebook.

On Friday afternoon, while Adina sleeps, Emilia quietly takes her suitcase out of the wardrobe and puts it down in the living room. It is two days before Gil leaves and four days before she joins him. Adina wakes up, and when she sees the suitcase she asks Emilia, 'Are you leaving?' Only then does Emilia realize that Hava hasn't told her about the trip.

She tells Adina in Hebrew, using hand gestures to simulate a plane flying, 'Not leaving. I'm going on trip. I'll come back after.' Adina nods, although Emilia isn't sure if she understands.

Her clothes are folded in a pile. They give off a smell of soap powder that manages to overpower the odour of sweat and dust in the old suitcase.

The next morning, on Saturday, shortly after they wake up and while Emilia is still in her pyjamas, Hava arrives with her husband, Meir, and their two children. They wait for Emilia to help Adina get dressed, and then Hava asks the kids to take Adina downstairs for tea in the lobby. She tells Emilia to stay so that she and Meir can talk to her.

They ask her to sit down in the living room, on the bed she has not yet had time to fold back into a sofa, and they sit opposite her on two chairs they bring in from the dining area. Emilia hasn't even had coffee yet. They tell her they know she's stealing money and jewellery from Adina and that she's planning to flee the country, and that if she doesn't give back everything she stole immediately, they're taking her straight to the police.

10

EMILIA WATCHES HERSELF OPEN the wardrobe in Adina's bedroom and take out her jewellery box and the little leather purse where Adina hides money. She puts the purse back and opens the jewellery box with the key and takes out a pair of pearl earrings. She doesn't know when or how the footage that Meir shows her on his phone was recorded. The clip is silent and the only sound Emilia can hear is Hava shouting: 'So you didn't steal from her, you little bitch?! You have the gall to lie to us?!' She informs Emilia that they have other footage too.

Meir is calmer. He gestures at Hava to stop yelling and puts his phone down on the table. He says to Emilia, 'If you'd like, we can settle this between ourselves. Pay her five thousand shekels and give back all the jewellery you took, and we won't have to get the police involved. That'll be the easiest way.' Hava is more upset than he is, or at least that is how she looks. She objects to Meir's offer. Even though he repeatedly asks her to lower her voice, she screams, 'Five thousand? Why? How do you know she didn't take more, the bitch? And where do you think she's going to come up with that money? Hey?' She threatens to tell the police that Emilia was abusing her mother. Meir says, 'So how much do you want her to pay? Ten thousand? If she gives you back ten thousand, will you let her off? I think it's better to settle this between us.' Then he adds, 'Perhaps you want to hear her side, Hava? Let's hear what she has to say.'

Emilia does not have much to say. Meir listens to her. She apologizes. She cries. She vehemently denies hitting Adina. How could they accuse her of that? She sits with Adina every night, holding her hand until she falls asleep. She explains that she was only borrowing the earrings and the necklace and she's already put them back. Everything is in the jewellery box, they can ask Adina if anything's missing. Meir looks as if he believes her: 'All right, we'll check.' But Hava says, 'You think Mum remembers what she did and didn't have? She can't remember anything! How exactly are we supposed to check?' Regarding the money, Emilia swears she hasn't taken anything for months. She insists she took only a hundred shekels at most, three or four times during her first few weeks. She explains that she was renting a flat and the part-time pay wasn't enough for rent, and that she'd promised herself she would give the money back when she could. She doesn't tell them that she could have already paid it back but whenever she had any money in her purse she put it in the donation basket at church or bought things for Gil's flat.

Hava raises her voice again: 'Now you're arguing with us?' She turns to Meir: 'She can explain all this to the police, not to me. And it's a good thing we took most of the money out of there, otherwise who knows how much she'd have left.' Meir speaks again: 'Don't argue with her, Emilia, I'm asking you. You're not in a position to argue with her. Pay her back seven thousand five hundred shekels by tomorrow and we'll part on good terms. I'll make sure she doesn't go to the police, okay? I'm telling you, I'm on your side and I don't want anyone to get in trouble, okay? Hava, are you listening? She'll pay you seven thousand five hundred and we'll put it to rest. Meanwhile, leave us your passport and everything you have here, and you'll get it all back when you bring the money – or from the police. It's your choice.'

WHEN EMILIA LEAVES THE nursing home for the last time, it's a little after 11 a.m. The lobby is full of caregivers and elderly people and relatives, and Emilia thinks they must all know what happened in the room on the seventh floor a few minutes ago, even though none of them can know and no one, including the receptionist, pays attention as she walks out of the lift and quickly crosses the hall to the sliding glass doors.

Emilia's belongings remain in Adina's flat. She had to give her passport and papers to Hava and Meir. She carries some clothes in her plastic bag. The long leather purse is there too. She wears her grey jeans and grey T-shirt and covers her eyes with the red sunglasses. Her denim jacket was also left behind.

Emilia walks from Bat Yam to the church in Jaffa, the same route she has taken many times. The walk seems longer. Slower. The day is bright and the sun is blazing. Everyone she comes across stares at her. She doesn't know where she will sleep that night or how she will get the money that Meir and Hava are demanding. She doesn't have the strength to go on living. She thinks of going back to the home when it gets dark and asking one of the caregivers to let her sleep there. She just wants to leave Israel and go home. She is afraid that if she tells Gil what happened, he will think she was stealing money from him, too, and perhaps from Esther and Nachum, even though she had never even considered doing that. She doesn't dare enter the church; instead she sits outside on a bench in the square full of tourists. Tadeusz will not come because he's with his family in Poland, and that is for the best because she could not have looked him in the eye after what has happened. Her skin burns with fear and shame. For what she has done – there is no forgiveness and never will be.

GIL CALLS HER IN the early evening, as if he knew she needed to talk to him. He can hear in her voice that something has gone wrong even before she says she cannot join him.

'But what happened, Emilia? Can you tell me?' Emilia doesn't answer. When he repeats the question she starts to sob. She cannot stop.

She tells him that Hava is accusing her of stealing money and jewellery and that she had to hand over her papers. That they asked her for money she does not have, and that if she doesn't get it to them by the next afternoon they will take her to the police. Gil listens quietly. He asks where she is and with who. When he offers to come to her place, there is no point in lying to him any more. She tells him that she has nowhere to sleep and no one other than he can help her. He asks if he can phone her back in a few minutes, and he calls after more than half an hour.

The sun is setting, evening is falling. Emilia's skin burns a little less, and the fear inside her has abated somewhat while she waited for Gil to phone. He says everything is going to be fine. He promises to help. He asks her to do exactly what he says. He wants her to take a bus and go to his flat. She debates taking a taxi but doesn't want anyone to see her or talk to her, and on the bus it's easier to hide. The bus is almost empty on a Saturday night, and Emilia sits on the seat nearest the back door, next to the window. She remembers her first bus ride to Gil's office, and seeing Tadeusz on the bus, perhaps at the station where she just got on, and how he'd stood without anyone offering him a seat. The ride goes quickly and no one sits next to her. When she gets off she knows she must go straight and then right. Gil's address is written in her notebook, which she left at Adina's, but Emilia remembers the way and recognizes the building. She doesn't turn on the light when she enters the building and walks up the steps in the dark, but when she stops outside his door, on the second floor, the stairwell light comes on, even though no other door opens or shuts and no one else goes up or down. She knocks twice and there is no answer, so she takes the key out of the fuse-box cupboard and goes in, as he told her to. The minute she enters she wants to lie down and shut her eyes. She is grateful for this place. She doesn't hear the door open and shut, perhaps because she nodded off, she simply feels his soft hand on her shoulder and sees him above her. In his other hand he holds a glass of water.

Afterwards they sit together at the dining table with the embroidered tablecloth Emilia had bought and the wicker basket from her old flat.

Gil waits for Emilia to recover, then instructs her to tell him exactly what happened. He asks her lots of question, and she answers. He asks if she took money from Adina and she swears she took no more than a few hundred shekels, and only in the first few weeks of working there, and that since she started working for him she hasn't taken even a shekel. She borrowed jewellery two or three times, when she went out with Gil in the evenings, and immediately put them back in the box. She can't explain why she took money from Adina because she has no explanation. She knows it's not because of the money but for other reasons, and the fact is, she never stole from Nachum and Esther. Gil says he believes her, but then he asks if she took something she shouldn't have taken from his flat, too, and she says never, and she swears she didn't take anything from Nachum and Esther either. Gil says quietly that he's not asking about his parents but about this flat – is she positive she never took something she shouldn't have? He strokes her hand to calm her nerves. He says he believes her and that he will help her. He asks if she told Meir and Hava who she's supposed to go to Riga with. He wants to call them to clarify that she wasn't planning to flee but is supposed to go away with him, and when she says she didn't tell them about him he says he will introduce himself. 'Anyway, whatever you did, they're not allowed to take your passport and certainly not to blackmail you like this,' he says, 'Let me talk to them and I promise they'll sing a different tune when they know they're talking with a lawyer.' Then he offers to make her a cup of tea and asks if she wants to have a shower. He goes to his bedroom to call Meir and Hava, but first he assures her, 'Everything is going to work out, Emilia, I promise. You're not alone.'

Emilia says she's sorry about the trip, and Gil smiles and says, 'It's no big deal, Emilia. There'll be other opportunities.'

As she stands under the stream of hot water in the shower she thinks about Nachum and shuts her eyes tight. From the shame and the sorrow. From the gratitude. She saw him in the living room earlier, when she walked into the flat in the dark, before Gil arrived, and she realized he was there for her. Since the day he died he had not left her.

When Emilia walks out of the bathroom, wearing the clothes she brought in the plastic bag, Gil says he's spoken with Hava and everything is going to be okay. He will settle the payment and they promised not to go to the police and to give her back her papers. Emilia asks how much money she will have to pay and Gil repeats that everything will be okay. He will pay them back, he doesn't want to say how much, but less than the seven thousand five hundred they were demanding. 'You have nothing to worry about,' he says, 'everything will be behind us. Tomorrow.'

He asks her to drink the tea he made while she was in the shower.

The tea tastes odd, too sweet, and it's gone cold, but Emilia drinks it all because she hasn't had anything to eat or drink all day. Gil walks her to his bedroom and she lies down, dizzy from exhaustion and from the overbearing heat. He sits next to her, watching her, the way she used to sit on Adina's bed and wait for her to fall asleep. The blinds are slightly open and light from the building across the way filters through, and in the dim light she sees Gil's face just before she falls asleep. He doesn't touch her. He sits next to her and she hears his voice. She thinks he is asking her something about Orna but she isn't sure because her mind is foggy. She remembers that she sometimes wondered what it would be like to wake up here, but she never imagined she would feel so good.

The bell she hung on the window does not move, but Emilia can hear its music. Her eyes shut and open and shut again, and she sees that Nachum is also in the bedroom and his green eyes are looking at her while she falls asleep. She wants to tell him something but she can't, because a weakness takes over her and her voice disappears from her mouth. She thinks he wants to tell her something, too, but he cannot move his lips either.

WHEN EMILIA WAKES UP at one o'clock, on the night between Saturday and Sunday, her plastic bag is covering her face, and when she tries to inhale she can taste the plastic in her mouth. She feels Gil's fingers pressing on both her knees, pinning them to the bed, preventing her from getting up, but Emilia doesn't want to get up, it's only the body that wants to. Her panic from the lack of air increases, yet somehow she also grows calmer.

Gil sits next to her. He watches Emilia as the air runs out of the bag.

Nachum is there, too, his eyes wide open, and Emilia realizes that Nachum was not trying to guide her to Gil, but to warn her.

Emilia's eyes are open, but inside she is shutting them. And all at once she knows everything that happened and also everything that is going to happen, as if it were a story told to her before the final sleep.

Three

I

HE WILL MEET THE third woman at the café in Givatayim where he once sat with you, Orna. She will come to the café every morning shortly after eight, and she will always sit at the same table in the corner of the patio that is glassed in for winter. He will come to the café half an hour after she gets there, at first not every morning but once or twice a week, on his way to the office.

Their first conversation will evolve this way: she will be sitting alone at her laptop, focused on her work but watching everyone who goes in and out. About once an hour she will get up and go outside to smoke and make a phone call, and on one of the mornings he will follow her out and ask for a cigarette. She will hand him a Winston Light from an almost empty white pack and he will light it for himself with her lighter. She will keep looking at her phone as he apologizes and says he hardly smokes, so he doesn't have his own, and she will say that she should stop, too, but maybe it's not the right time because she just took it up. He will laugh. He will say he'd like to ask her something, and she will put her phone in her coat pocket and tell him that's fine. Only then will she look up at him. He will ask, 'What are you working on so seriously in there every morning?' Then, to be polite, she will ask him what he does.

When they go back into the café he will hold out his hand and introduce himself. 'I'm Gil, by the way,' he'll say, and she'll reply, 'Nice to meet you, I'm Ella.'

FROM THAT DAY ON he will stop by almost every morning. His face is smooth and he smells of cologne and wears a different shirt every day. His hair is a little sparser than you both remember, but still fair and quite full. He will park in the car park nearby and walk to the café. The second time he follows her out and asks for a cigarette, their conversation will be longer. The first thing that will bring them together is the topic of the thesis she is trying to write, even though – she will tell him – she doesn't think she's ever going to finish it, not at her age. 'What are you writing about?' he will ask, and she will answer, 'Forget it, you don't really want to know.'

She is writing about the Łódź Ghetto. Yes, about 'the Holocaust.' Actually about one single building in the Łódź Ghetto between 1941 and 1944, and the lives of the people who lived there during those years. Dozens of residents, dozens of completely different stories, dozens of deaths, each more tragic than the other. And she's thirty-seven, not an age when you're supposed to be writing university papers. She is older than most of the professors and looks like all the other students' mothers.

Gil will seem surprised by her topic, because she doesn't look like that's where she's from, and she will laugh and call him a racist, but then she'll say that actually she isn't – is it so obvious? She will explain that her interest in the topic began during her army service, when she taught history to soldiers in the Education Corps, and then went on to study Jewish History at Bar Ilan University. After that she worked at the Museum of the Diaspora for a few years, as a guide for tourist groups.

'And now?' he will ask. 'Now I mostly have babies,' she will say, puffing her cigarette smoke away from him. Her last one was born ten months ago, and so as not to go crazy she signed up for an MA and hired a nanny who watches the baby at home, every morning and one afternoon a week, but it's not really helping. 'Not helping because you still don't have enough time for your studies?' Gil will ask, and she will say, 'Not helping because I'm still going crazy. And I don't really know why I'm even doing this.'

She also has two older girls, four and a half and six, and taking care of the three of them drives her mad. Those few hours in the morning and the full day at university are her salvation, but they're not enough to maintain her sanity. Without the SSRIs and without taking up smoking again, after almost seven years without a cigarette, since she first got pregnant – she will say as she lights another Winston Light – she wouldn't make it. Her husband is a career soldier, he does research, and he doesn't get home until after nine. 'I'm not sure he even knows we had another baby,' she will say, taking out her phone to show him pictures of the girls. 'Don't get me wrong, I love all three of them, they're real sweethearts,' she will add, 'but this is not how I imagined my life ten years ago. But why am I even sharing all this with you? It's all to avoid going back to work, I suppose.'

AND THIS TIME IT will be clear right from the start that they're both married.

Gil will have a thin wedding ring that he will not take off before entering the café and will not try to hide from her, and she will talk about her husband a lot.

They will start to say good morning to each other when he gets to the café and she is already there and he asks her for a cigarette for the third and fourth times, and after that she will beckon to him every time she goes out to smoke. On rainy days they will huddle under the shelter of a nearby bodega and on cold days they will stand on the pavement near the café door to get some of the warmth from the kerosene heater inside. If it's a nice day they will sit at the round table set out for smokers, and they will enjoy the sunshine. February will be dry, and early on in the month there will be warm days in which summer is folded like stamens in a flower. He will offer to buy her a pack of cigarettes or pay for her coffee because she can't keep financing his new habit, and she will say: on the contrary, she feels guilty because it's her fault he's smoking more.

And to her he will not lie. He will tell her that he has two daughters, one doing her army service at the Air Force training base, the other finishing high school soon, and that his wife is also a lawyer. He will not say Ruthi's name but he will also not claim that they are divorced or getting divorced. When she asks, 'How is it that she never comes here with you?' he will explain that she leaves for work before he does, and that her office is in central Tel Aviv. His Eastern European connections will continue to be a common denominator. He will say that his father was born in Austria and his mother in Poland, not in Lodz but in a little town near Warsaw named Grójec. They both died recently: his father, Nachum, died almost three years ago and his mother, Esther, at the end of summer, after Rosh Hashanah.

He will tell her more about his work and she will take an interest: what sort of people apply for Romanian or Polish or Bulgarian citizenship, and why? How did he end up doing that kind of work? He will explain that in the mid-nineties he worked for an employment agency and built up good contacts when they were bringing over a lot of cheap labour to Israel – mostly women – from Eastern Europe, after the fall of the Communist Bloc, and after that he opened his own firm. At first, when the Eastern European countries had just entered the EU, he mostly worked on passport applications, because Israelis love being able to stand in the EU lines at airports around Europe. But now most of his work is on real-estate investments. Israelis are buying more and more property in Eastern Europe, as if they're planning to go back there en masse one day, and since they don't trust the local lawyers, his business is booming. He also has three of his own profitable properties in Eastern Europe, and he's currently exploring partnerships in two big projects, which is why he travels a lot, sometimes twice a month, and he's hired three lawyers to work for him, one here, one in Romania and one in Poland.

'Sounds busy and flourishing, unlike my life,' she will say. When he remarks, 'Let's not exaggerate. The fact is, I still have time to come here for coffee with you every morning,' she will look at him and smile. She will say, 'So that's what you're saying? That you come here to have coffee with me?'

When he asks why she chose her thesis topic, she will reply, 'I honestly don't know any more. I used to be ambitious. And I felt that the people who died there were asking me not to forget.'

2

EMILIA'S BODY WAS FOUND early on a Sunday morning near the old central bus station in south Tel Aviv. The report filed by Sergeant Kareem Nasri, the patrol officer who found her, said this: 'Deceased female in her forties. Short hair, dressed in grey trousers and T-shirt. Lying in stairwell of building on Ha'Galil Street. Head covered with plastic bag.' No identifying papers or other documents were found on her, and so for several days she remained unidentified.

Since there were no signs of violence on Emilia, the initial assumption was suicide. An autopsy determined the cause of death as suffocation. 'She did not have sexual intercourse in the hours preceding her death and there were virtually no traces of food in her stomach.' The report also stated that the woman was likely not Israeli, based on the type of crowns in her teeth; her clothing labels matched this assumption. The time of death was estimated as early in the night between Saturday and Sunday.

For a few days the investigation focused on scanning the area where Emilia was found, questioning local residents and comparing the report findings to missing-person cases. There were few cameras in the area, and none had recorded Emilia in the hours before her death. Police officers showed her picture to business owners and residents in nearby streets, but no one recognized her. Searches of gardens and rubbish bins found no items or papers that might have belonged to her.

Emilia was labelled 'anonymous' in the police reports, and one conjecture offered but quickly rejected was that she'd been smuggled into Israel to work in prostitution, perhaps without her consent. But none of the women at known prostitution houses in the neighbourhood recognized Emilia, and her physical condition also contradicted this hypothesis. Emilia was malnourished, but she had not been using drugs and showed no signs of abuse.

THE IDENTIFICATION WAS MADE more than a week later.

A complaint was filed at Ayalon Precinct in Bat Yam against a foreign caregiver who had stolen money and abused the elderly woman she cared for in a nursing home, before vanishing. Perhaps she'd fled the country. The couple who filed the complaint, Meir and Hava Yashar, gave the on-duty investigator the caregiver's name and description, and a few days later someone at the precinct connected the dots. The Yashars were called to the police station on Ha'Masger Street to look at the photograph of the anonymous deceased woman, and they immediately identified her: Emilia Nodyeves, a Latvian citizen, forty-six years old. She had cared for Adina Denino since the end of January and lived in her flat at the nursing home in Bat Yam since 1 March. She'd entered Israel legally more than two years prior, through the mediation of an employment agency, and her visa and work permit were in order.

When the Yashars were asked when they'd last seen Emilia, they said Saturday morning – several hours before her estimated time of death. They said they'd suspected Emilia was stealing money from the lady she cared for and had installed hidden cameras that had confirmed their suspicions. On Saturday they'd surprised her by showing her the footage. They had not threatened her, only asked her to give back the money. They might have also warned her that they would go to the police, they said.

They claimed Emilia had promised to give the money back that same day, then she'd left the nursing home and hadn't been heard of since. They knew she had been planning a trip overseas in a few days and so had asked her to leave her passport with them. Two days after she disappeared they got in touch with the employment agency, but no one there had any idea where Emilia was. The Yashars thought she had somehow managed to leave the country without her passport and they had come to terms with the loss of money. They'd filed the complaint only because they realized they had to in order to demand compensation from the agency for the damages caused by Emilia.

When asked if they had anything else that belonged to Emilia Nodyeves, other than her passport, they said no, just some clothes that were still on the shelves in Adina's bedroom and a few toiletries in the bathroom.

AFTER THE IDENTIFICATION OF the body and the Yashars' testimony, the case was virtually clear to the police investigators. The Yashars' story had reinforced the assumption that Emilia had committed suicide, and enabled the investigators to outline the hours preceding her death. She'd left the nursing home in the morning, after her confrontation with Meir and Hava, unable to leave Israel because her passport had been confiscated. She was afraid to go back to the home in case they took her to the police, and she spent the whole day wandering alone in search of a way out. She had nowhere to sleep. They weren't sure why or how she'd gone from Bat Yam all the way to Neveh Sha'anan in south Tel Aviv, or if she had social or other connections there, but by night-time her desperation had apparently increased and she had decided to take her own life. One theory was that she'd gone to south Tel Aviv to look for work in the local prostitution houses to make some money, but perhaps she'd changed her mind at the last minute.

The first detective put in charge of the case was Inspector A., an investigation officer at Tel Aviv South Precinct. Aged forty-one, married with six children, a former border patrol officer, resident of Yehud. He was a tall, thin man with a slow and measured demeanour and tired eyes. He was convinced that Emilia had suffocated herself out of despair and fear, but since he was a thorough investigator and prided himself on always filing meticulous reports, he wanted to tie up the loose ends regarding Emilia's final day: How was it possible that no one had seen her around the central bus station in the hours before her suicide? After all, there was even a police station not far from there.

Inspector A. called the Yashars in for another interview, to get a more complete picture of what had happened that Saturday morning at the nursing home. He did not view them as suspects, but he did think they might not be disclosing everything about what had transpired. At his request, they brought a flash drive with footage of Emilia opening Adina's wardrobe and removing jewellery and money. He watched it several times and asked them to let him keep it. In the original complaint they'd filed, they'd also claimed Emilia had abused Adina, but the footage from the hidden camera contained no evidence of this and in their second interview they retracted their accusation.

Their testimony depicted a lonely woman with no relatives or friends in Israel. The Yashars knew she had previously worked as a caregiver in north Tel Aviv, and that she'd lived for a few weeks in a rented flat in Bat Yam before moving into the home. She worked six days a week and had requested and received Sundays off, so that she could run errands and go to church. She had recently asked for a few days' leave to travel to Riga, and only in retrospect had they realized that she must have been planning to leave Israel and not return. Inspector A. asked if it was possible that Adina knew any more details about her, but they told him she was in a very disoriented state.

*

ONE MORNING, ALMOST A month after the body was found, Inspector A. went directly from the synagogue in Yehud where he said prayers every morning to the nursing home in Bat Yam, where he questioned employees, both Israeli and foreign, who added no significant information about the circumstances surrounding Emilia's death. No one knew much about her; she'd been reclusive and withdrawn. A Filipina worker named Jenny told him she'd seen Emilia at the church in Jaffa, and another worker named Carol, whom Inspector A. thought looked very masculine despite her long hair, said she'd recently seen Emilia leave the home in the evenings, dressed for a date. Carol couldn't say who Emilia was meeting and if she had an intimate relationship with a man or a woman. None of them came to her funeral, which was held in Israel because no one in Latvia asked for the body, and none of them had since come across anyone in the nursing home asking about Emilia or wondering how she was.

Inspector A. was planning to go to his office, but he decided to stop at the church in Jaffa, following the testimonies of the Filipina worker and the Yashars. It was a Sunday, and he got there just before one o'clock, after a quick and overpriced lunch in a beachside café. He entered the church without removing the yarmulke from his head, even though when he'd visited Notre-Dame in Paris with his wife once he'd taken it off in the large square outside the cathedral. A priest led Inspector A. to a small room behind the colourful, bright prayer hall and asked him to wait. The priest thought he recognized Emilia from the photograph Inspector A. showed him. He returned with three other priests, one of whom identified Emilia definitively and said he'd known her well. His name was Tadeusz, and he was the first person who seemed grief-stricken to learn of Emilia's death.

They sat down at a table in the little room, and Tadeusz told Inspector A. that he used to sit with Emilia right at that very table almost every Sunday for a talk. He said she'd started coming to Mass three or four months ago and had approached him after prayers one day and asked to talk. She needed advice, someone to talk to, and they'd had some very intimate conversations.

Inspector A. wondered if the priest sitting before him might be the person Emilia went out to meet every so often in the evenings. He was young and very handsome, and Inspector A. did not believe that priests and rabbis had no urges and desires, especially not since he and his wife had watched the movie *Spotlight*. For a moment, Inspector A. even went so far as to consider asking the priest where he'd been on the night Emilia died, because he thought she might have come to him for help after she was thrown out of the nursing home. But the Polish priest beat him to it, explaining that he hadn't seen Emilia in the weeks preceding her death, first because she'd avoided him, or at least so it had seemed, and then because he'd gone to visit his family in Poland. Besides, he was the first person who insisted that Emilia could not have committed suicide. She had lived a very lonely life, the priest said, but she was on a journey of discovery, and unless something extremely unusual had happened in the two weeks before she died, he had trouble believing she could have suffocated herself. He wanted to know where Emilia was buried, was surprised to hear that it was in Israel and not Latvia, and asked Inspector A. if he could tell him where the grave was located so that he could visit and lay flowers.

When Inspector A. told Tadeusz that Emilia had stolen money from the woman she cared for, the priest said nothing. Inspector A. pressed him, asking if he'd known about it, and Tadeusz said softly, 'No, but I might have suspected something.' He'd noticed Emilia putting large amounts of money in the donation basket that was passed around after prayers, and said she'd refused to come to confession even though he'd urged her to, as if she had something to hide. But he thought the money might have been coming from somewhere else, and that Emilia was hiding other things from him, not theft.

When asked if Emilia had told him about anyone she was in touch with, apart from the lady she cared for, the priest remarked that in the weeks before her death she had hinted at a relationship with a man whose flat she cleaned – that was where he thought she was getting the money. He didn't know much about the man, except that he was the son of the old man Emilia had cared for before she moved to the nursing home, and that she cleaned his home on Sundays, before church. When Tadeusz asked if this man had been questioned, Inspector A. said no and made a note to himself. That afternoon he called Emilia's employment agency and was given Nachum and Esther's home phone number.

He called them a little after five, just as Father Tadeusz was preparing for weekly Mass and deciding to dedicate it to Emilia's memory and say a few words about his meetings with her and about her life and death.

Esther was the first person who actually cried when she heard about Emilia's death. She said, 'My Emilia, I shouldn't have let her go. I knew she should have stayed with me.' She was surprised when Inspector A. said he understood Emilia had been cleaning her son's house until shortly before her death and asked for his phone number.

'You mean Ze'ev? Or Gil?' Esther asked. 'They didn't tell me she was working for them.'

She gave him both phone numbers, and first he phoned the wrong brother.

3

ONE MORNING GIL WILL suggest that she has lunch with him, and she will say no. He will ask why and she will say, 'Because you know it's a bad idea. It's nice meeting like this, so why ruin it? I think there are lines we shouldn't cross, don't you?'

He will back off, but for a few days he will not come to the café in the mornings. When he returns she will ask, 'So that's that? It's either lunch or nothing?' He will pretend to be surprised, act as if he'd forgotten about asking her out for lunch, and explain that he was on a work trip. 'But maybe we could have lunch some time after all?' he'll add, and she will laugh and say, 'Are you really hungry?' Later that morning, just before he gets up to leave for work, she will go over to his table and say, 'You know what? Okay. Lunch, but early. I'll ask the nanny if there's a day when she can stay until two or three. And it's my treat.' He will smile and ask if she's sure and she will say, 'Yes, fuck it, why not,' but will add that they'll have to meet somewhere there's no chance of running into her husband.

A WEEK LATER AT the Jaffa port. Wednesday, early March.

They will arrange to meet there because her husband's base is in north Tel Aviv, on the other side of town, and they will each get there on their own. She will look completely different, in a blue dress that hugs her hips and flares above the knees, because it will be a hot day, almost a heatwave, and she will wear heels, and from far away she will suddenly remind him of Orna. She is not pretty but there will be something winning about the way she walks and the way she picks up her wine glass and looks at Gil and then lowers her eyes when she has nothing to say.

They will eat at a fish restaurant in the port and, despite the spring weather and the view of the old fishing boats in the marina and the option to smoke, they will not sit on the deck but inside, so as not to be seen. After lunch they will take a short walk along the port, heading north, to the clock tower just near Tadeusz's church. She will say that she hasn't been there for years, and Gil will look at her and say that he also can't remember the last time he was there either.

At the beginning of the meal they will share moments of silence, almost awkwardness. As if beyond the café and the quick cigarette breaks they have nothing to say to one another. She will apparently decide that the way to break the ice is to be direct, even blunt, so she will say, 'So, tell me how long you've been cheating on your wife.'

Gil will be surprised but not alarmed. He will smile. 'Wow, that's quite a way to start a conversation.' And then he will say, 'It's been a few years. But it's very infrequent, despite what you may think.'

'What's very infrequent?' she will ask, and he will insist he's had no more than two or three flings, or acquaintances with women that developed into something you might call a relationship.

'Doesn't your wife suspect anything?'

He will say she probably does. She likely knows and turns a blind eye. She has no choice because even though she also works, she's financially dependent on him. Then he'll ask about her and she'll put her wine glass to her lips as she shakes her head and says, 'Never.' She will add that up until a year or two ago she couldn't even contemplate it.

'Then why are you here?' he will ask, and she'll say, 'Because this isn't a year or two ago. And I'm still not sure I know why I'm here. Maybe curiosity.'

'Curiosity about what?'

'I can't say exactly. About you? You strike me as a strange man, Gil. Really strange. But more likely it's about me. Curiosity about what I can and cannot do. Or more importantly, what I can or cannot feel.'

When Gil asks her to explain what she means and what she finds strange about him, she will become evasive and say that several of her friends cheat on their husbands and talk about it with great excitement, but that she'll probably never be able to do it. 'Avner is the most jealous man in the world, there's no way he would live with it.'

'But what can he do to you?' Gil will ask, and she will say, 'I don't want to think about that, okay? He'll just break everything up. He'll never forgive me. Isn't that scary enough?'

FOR A WHILE THEY will talk about other things.

When Gil mentions that their waitress reminds him of Noa, she will ask about his relationship with his daughters, and he will say that it's always been great and is only getting better as the girls get older. Noa doesn't have a boyfriend right now, so when she comes home from the army at weekends they sometimes go to the movies, and a couple of weeks ago they even went to a bar together. Hadass is insanely busy with exams and she's more of a mummy's girl, but he's very close to her too.

He will order himself another glass of wine and say he's decided not to go back to the office after lunch. For his entrée he will have sea bass with rice and green beans, and she will have a salad. He will ask about her relationship with her daughters and also with her father, but very soon they will resume talking about affairs, when she starts questioning him on the practicalities: How does he do it? He will say that usually, after the initial acquaintance stage, which happens online or sometimes in other ways, they meet in a hotel in Tel Aviv or Herzliya, or at a B&B that lets rooms by the hour. But he also has a flat in Givatayim, which for the past year he's been renting to tourists on Airbnb, and sometimes, mostly in winter, it sits empty. With longer relationships they sometimes even go overseas, for a weekend in nearby destinations like Athens or Cyprus or Bucharest – quick, inexpensive getaways that the women can easily disguise as shopping or work trips.

She will listen with focus, like a girl hearing the most important thing ever told to her for the first time in her life. When she says, 'But why do you need it, actually? Explain that to me,' he will say, 'I don't need it. It just happens. I mean, it doesn't make sense that it should stop just because we get married and grow a bit older, does it?'

'What should stop?'

'Wanting to meet new people. To get close to them. What turns me on is not the sex but the getting close. The true intimacy you suddenly have with someone new, whom you didn't know before and who is gradually revealed to you. That's what's exciting, isn't it?'

The restaurant will be practically empty during their meal, and by the time they have dessert and coffee there will be no other diners there. Gil will ask if he can put his hand on hers and she will say yes, and his soft, damp hand will stay on hers for several minutes, hiding her wedding ring. She will not resist. She will say to him quietly, 'Do you understand that no one apart from my husband has touched me for more than ten years?'

AFTER THEIR SHORT STROLL, Gil will walk her to her car, which will be parked in the sandy car park near the clock tower square. It will be almost three o'clock.

He will ask if she's sure she doesn't want to come over to his empty flat or go to a hotel with him, now or any other time she chooses. She will say that she's late for the nanny. She will open the car door and put her handbag on the passenger seat and then look at him and say, 'I had a good time, really, but I'm afraid this is as much as you're going to get out of me, Gil. Or as much as I'll get out of myself, I don't know. I don't think I can do it. As it is, what's happened is a lot more than I meant to happen.' He will smile and say, 'As long as we keep having a cigarette together sometimes, it's all good. After all, now I'm addicted.'

When they move in for a goodbye hug he will seek her lips and find them, and when she responds for an instant they will kiss. In the following weeks he will treat her differently. He will be bolder, more desperate, he will hardly lie, he will not give up easily when she says no. As if he is not the same Gil you both knew, or as if time has changed him too.

4

THE POLICE REPORT STATED that Attorney Gil Hamtzani was summoned to provide initial testimony concerning the death of Emilia Nodyeves approximately six weeks after her body was found on Ha'Galil Street. He came to Tel Aviv South Precinct on Ha'Masger Street at 11 a.m. and was questioned by Inspector A., the investigating officer overseeing the case, in his office on the second floor. The summary of the testimony, written in Inspector A.'s handwriting and signed by Gil, was added to the growing investigation file, at the bottom of which was an enlarged photograph of Emilia's face, taken on the early Sunday morning when she was found, after the removal of the plastic bag from her head.

GIL CONFIRMED RIGHT AT the start of his testimony that he had known Emilia.

She had cared for his father for two years, and he met her when he visited his parents and at family events. He was not involved in her employment – the person who handled that was his brother Ze'ev – and he had never talked with her privately while she'd worked for his parents. To the best of his knowledge she had done her job well, and his father and mother had been pleased with her. He had known nothing about her at the time except that she was Latvian. And he thought she was older than she really was, forty-eight or fifty.

A few weeks after his father's death, Emilia had contacted him at his office, on Esther's recommendation. She needed legal counsel about her work permit and visa, and he had given her the advice pro bono, because of his mother's request.

'What was the problem? Why did she need advice?' Inspector A. asked, and Gil explained that Emilia wanted to take another job, in addition to caring for the old lady at the nursing home where the agency had placed her. She wanted to know if she could do so with her current work permit, or if she could amend the permit issued by the Ministry of the Interior before she'd come to Israel. She explained that she needed extra income urgently, and he had the impression, from both her behaviour and her appearance, that she was in severe distress.

'What sort of distress? Can you describe it?' Inspector A. sat up straight in his chair and leaned closer to Gil. The things Gil said matched the assumptions he was developing at that very minute. He had the sense that Gil's testimony could fill in several gaps in the case.

'Financial distress, but perhaps emotional too. I can't tell you exactly. I got the feeling she needed money urgently, maybe even a lot of money, to pay debts or send money abroad, I don't know. So I gave her some work for a few weeks, even though I knew it was illegal—'

'We'll get to that soon,' Inspector A. interjected. 'Do you remember what you advised her to do in that meeting?'

'I explained to her that she couldn't work at another job on her existing permit, and that it would be hard to change but I could try. And she asked me to try. I recommended that in the meantime she ask the employment agency for more work, but she said they weren't giving her anything. She asked what would happen if she cleaned houses without reporting it and if they could deport her – she was absolutely unwilling to go back to Riga. I explained that they could, but it's true that a few weeks later, when she called to find out if I'd managed to change the permit, I suggested she come and clean for me.'

AT THE BOTTOM OF Gil's testimony, in the neat handwriting that had characterized him since he'd been in primary school in Nazareth, Inspector A. added a few questions that still bothered him after hearing what the lawyer had had to say: *Who was she sending money to in Latvia? Why was she planning to go to Riga if she was so afraid of being sent back there? Was she mixed up in something financially or legally over there?* Then he wrote himself a reminder and underlined it: *Talk to the consulate again.*

He asked Gil when Emilia had called him the second time and what exactly she'd asked for, and Gil said it was two or three weeks after she visited his office. She wanted to know if he'd been able to change her work permit, and he apologized and said he hadn't. When he asked what she was going to do, she said she had no choice but to risk taking illegal cleaning jobs. She asked if he knew anyone looking for a cleaner, because she'd rather work for people she knew and could trust, and not put up signs with her name and phone number. At first he said he didn't, but towards the end of the conversation, because of how distressed she sounded, he suggested she clean his flat. He had an investment property in Givatayim and it was empty at the time, in between renters and with a planned remodel, and he needed someone to clean it periodically. The main reason he suggested it was because he felt sorry for her and because of the close ties she'd had with his parents. When Inspector A. asked why he didn't tell Esther that Emilia had started working for him, Gil said he didn't want Esther to know that Emilia was in such a bad state.

Inspector A. asked when exactly Emilia had started working for him, and Gil said he couldn't remember the exact date and probably did not have it written down. He explained that at first she'd come to his office, in Ramat Gan, and he'd driven her to the flat and shown her exactly what to clean and how.

'And how did she look then? Was there any change from how you remembered her?'

'I think so. Although, as I told you, I hadn't seen her much before, so I'm not sure. She looked thin, almost emaciated, and as if she was under a lot of stress. As I said, she seemed very distraught.'

When Inspector A. asked how many times she'd cleaned his flat,

Gil said he would estimate six to eight times. Roughly once every two weeks. They set up the work times on short phone calls that Gil made to Emilia's mobile phone – a device the police had not found. Gil said he'd only seen her once in all those weeks, when he went to the flat to wait for a contractor who was giving him a bid for the refurbishment, and Emilia had just finished cleaning. Usually he left her the key in the fuse-box cupboard, with cash in an envelope, and she put the key back when she was done.

'Weren't you afraid to leave her the key?'

'No. Why should I have been?'

'And you never met her anywhere else? In the evening, perhaps?'

'Why would I meet her in the evening?'

'I don't know why, I'll ask and you answer,' said Inspector A., even though the idea of Gil meeting Emilia outside of work struck him, too, as unreasonable.

'Of course not. But I'm trying to understand why you're asking. After all, you don't ask questions for no reason. Do you suspect me of something?'

'I'm asking because I have testimony that she was going out with a man, and you're telling me she worked in your flat, and I want to understand if the two things are connected.'

Gil smiled. He said, 'No, I was definitely not "going out" with Emilia, as you call it. You can ask my wife if you'd like. That time I went to the flat and she was there, I gave her a ride south because I was on my way to a meeting in Jaffa. But other than that I never saw her outside the flat.'

‘Did she tell you anything? About her situation? Maybe about a partner or family in Israel or Latvia? About other flats she cleaned?’

Gil thought for a moment.

Then he said that to the best of his memory Emilia hadn’t mentioned any other workplace or any relative or boyfriend, but that he was under the impression that she needed money desperately because she was sending everything she made to a partner or a lover, or maybe even a child, in Riga. But she might have been giving it to a boyfriend in Israel.

‘Why do you think so? Did she hint at anything like that?’

‘No, I don’t remember anything specific. It was my impression, from our brief talks and from her appearance, that she needed money urgently. Judging by the clothes she wore and the way she looked, I don’t think she spent the money she made on herself.’

When Inspector A. told him that Emilia had been caught stealing from the lady she worked for at the nursing home in Bat Yam, Gil looked astonished but then he smiled. He said on the one hand it surprised him, because he’d never heard a complaint from his mother and father about anything like that, but on the other hand he wasn’t all that shocked because he’d often thought it was a good thing he didn’t have anything valuable at the flat, and that she seemed so desperate that she’d be willing to do anything for money.

Inspector A. got the hint: ‘What do you mean, anything?’

Gil said he wasn’t sure but he thought that when he took her to the flat the first time she’d hinted that she was willing to do ‘more than cleaning' for him. He wasn't positive that was what she was insinuating, and anyway he wasn't interested, of course.

Inspector A. looked at him for a moment, then made a note. 'Do you think her distress was so severe that she would have offered herself at the massage parlours or tried to pick up prostitution work on the street?'

Gil said he had no idea but it was possible. He asked if Inspector A. thought that was why Emilia had committed suicide, because she'd been caught stealing and because of the financial distress, and Inspector A. nodded. 'I assume it's related,' he said, 'but we still don't have enough information about her from the Latvians. It looks like financial and emotional distress, loneliness, alienation, fear of being arrested because of the theft and also because of working illegally, maybe fear of being deported back to Riga. From what you're telling me and from other testimonies, it's also possible that she had significant debt, here or perhaps in Latvia, or that she was financing someone overseas and was afraid she wouldn't be able to keep doing that because she'd no longer be able to work. It's very common with these women. I'm also not ruling out that she was so desperate she was willing to prostitute herself, which happens to a lot of women who come from there, and she couldn't live with it. We come across a lot of these stories. Especially in that screwed-up area around the central bus station.'

WHEN GIL LEFT HIS office, Inspector A. called the Latvian consulate again to find out if there were any more details from the Riga police about Emilia, but there was no answer because it was Sunday. He was fairly certain that he understood the circumstances surrounding her suicide and just wanted to fill in some gaps so that the story of her death would be complete. He put the photograph of Emilia's face into a plastic bag and straightened out the documents, because he didn't like it when papers stuck out of the white cardboard file and their edges got crumpled. Then he put the file on the corner of his desk, on top of a pile of other folders, and that was the last work he did on the case.

5

GIL WILL CONTINUE TO come to the café on Katznelson Street every morning, but she will not be there. He will wait for her, look up from his newspaper or phone every time he hears the door open, but the table where she sat will remain orphaned. Towards half past nine or quarter to ten, he will give up and go to work. On his way home, in the late afternoon, he will stop by the café again.

When a week has gone by since their date, he will decide not to keep waiting and that he will phone her from his office. It will be in the morning, shortly after the time they usually met at the café, and she will pick up immediately.

'Hello, Ella?' he will say, because he won't be sure the number he called is really hers, and he will have trouble recognizing her voice from her first 'hello'. She will not reply immediately but will pause for a moment, because she will recognize his voice. He will be trying to explain why he's calling when she cuts him off and asks,

'How did you get my number?' He will say that he heard her give it to someone on the phone and he couldn't resist writing it down, and she will ask him not to call her and will say she has to hang up. He will say, 'Can you at least explain why? Did I do something wrong?' and she will quickly answer that no, she can't talk but she hasn't been coming to the café because her nanny is sick and she's home with the girls. She will urge him again not to call her and will promise to get back to him when she can.

He will not believe what she says about being home with the girls and the nanny's illness. In the background there will be no crying or other babies' voices, but phones ringing and noises that make him think she's in a public space.

Her avoidance and the fact that she didn't get back to him as promised will anger him and he will call her again that evening. A little after ten, when her husband should be home. She will not answer and he will wait more than ten rings to leave her a message, but there will be no voicemail and eventually he will hang up. The next morning, to his utter surprise, he will see her at the café, sitting in her spot in the corner of the deck still covered with glass. She will motion for him to go out for a smoke as soon he walks in, and when they stand next to each other on the pavement outside the door, she will whisper, 'Are you mad? Why are you calling me when you know my husband's home? Are you trying to kill me?'

He will be wearing jeans and a blue shirt that morning, exactly the same clothes he wore to his first date with you, Orna, at Ha'Bima Square, and she will be wearing a light but not thin windbreaker, zipped up to her neck, and will not unzip it even though the morning clouds will scatter and the day will warm up. Gil will explain that he didn't understand why she'd stopped coming and he had to know. He thought they'd had a good date. She'd left him feeling that this was something they shouldn't miss out on. She will shush him and whisper, 'Are you seriously talking about these things right here out loud?!' At the smokers' table outside the café there will be a tall, unshaven man in black Adidas sweatpants talking on his phone, and the looks he throws at them will trouble both of them. They will move away and stand near the window of a still-shut real-estate office, and after she lights herself a cigarette and takes a drag she will tell him in her usual voice, but curtly, that she felt the same way. The day after their lunch her nanny really had been sick, as she'd told him, and she'd had to stay at home with the little one for two days, and it was those two days that had made her start thinking about what she'd done and she'd grown anxious. She'd decided not to go back to the café for a while and had gone somewhere else, hoping it would all fade away.

They will stand with their backs to the street, both reflected in the window, between the square for-sale signs with photographs of empty properties. When Gil tries to touch her hand again, as he had in Jaffa, she will put her hand into her coat pocket and hiss, 'What's the matter with you? Are you an idiot?'

'I know it's irrational,' she will tell him later, 'but I sit there at home and I have the feeling my husband knows. I'm sure he knows. I feel like he's looking at me differently. And then I look at my girls and I panic, do you understand? I don't think you can understand because your girls are older. I imagine what happens when he finds out and how everything falls apart in front of my eyes. And then I also think about you and about our morning cigarettes and our talks and our meeting in Jaffa and I want it, you know, I really want it, and I tell myself I haven't done anything wrong, goddammit, I haven't done anything, all I did was talk to someone who finally took an interest in my work and my life, so what am I panicking about, why am I frightened by myself and by him, can you explain that to me?'

When they go back inside they will each sit in their spot, but threads of looks and a wordless conversation will connect the two tables. Gil will text her: 'Don't give up on me, Ella,' and will watch her expression as she reads his message and smiles. She will write back, 'Please don't send me messages. Definitely not this kind. You can email if you want. I'm deleting your number and blocking it!' When he texts, 'What's your email address?' she will write back, 'Just send me yours.'

A few minutes later he will get a blank email from ella_hazany333@gmail.com and will immediately write back from his phone: 'So are we meeting tomorrow or tonight?' She will smile when she reads it and send back a reply a few minutes later: 'Not today or tomorrow. By the way, do you know I haven't written a word all week because of you? And I have a seminar paper due! (I can't believe I'm writing that, at my age.)'

For a few days they will keep emailing back and forth in the café, from two nearby tables, like kids in class passing notes back and forth without the teacher seeing. Gil will write to her during the day from his office too. He will ask if she was able to write that morning, how the seminar paper's going and what it's about, how her afternoon with the girls was and if she misses him. He will offer to get them a room for the morning at a hotel in Tel Aviv. When she writes, 'You're not serious, are you? How about getting us a room right outside my husband's office?' he will suggest other places.

He will ask if she's told anyone about him, and she will say there's nothing to tell and that even if there was she wouldn't do that. He will write that he told his older daughter, Noa, about her when she came home from the army at the weekend, which will not be true, because even with her he won't be able to resist lying sometimes.

And it'll be in one of those emails that he will first suggest the idea of them going overseas together.

6

THE INVESTIGATION INTO EMILIA'S death was forgotten, even though the case was still officially open. Shortly after questioning Gil, Inspector A. left his position at Tel Aviv South Precinct, at his request, and began a new promotion track in Sharon Precinct, which he believed would make him a station commander by the age of forty-five. In the induction meeting with his replacement, a good-looking detective still in his twenties, whose eyes looked vacant and emotionless, Inspector A. summed up the case as follows: 'Definite suicide of a foreign worker with no relatives in Israel. All questioning was completed, the case awaits answers to questions I sent the Riga police via the Latvian consulate, but apparently their staff is even slower than ours. As far as I'm concerned, when the answers arrive the case can be closed for good.'

TIME PASSED QUICKLY, EVEN if not your time, which never changes at all.

Babies were born, sick and elderly people died, among them Adina. She died at the nursing home, in the bed where Emilia had sat stroking her arm, watched over by her new caregiver, a Filipina named Rosie Christine. A few weeks later, when Hava went to the police station on Ha'Masger Street with a cardboard box containing Emilia's belongings, the desk sergeant did not know where to send her. The young detective overseeing the case was out, so she asked Hava to wait for the duty officer.

Hava put Emilia's box down by her feet and waited her turn. There was a cooking show on the television screen on the wall, and since the wait was much longer than she'd expected, she considered giving up on the whole thing and leaving. She thought this was unnecessary anyway, and Meir had agreed, but the man ahead of her, who had come to report the theft of gas canisters from his back garden, gave up his spot in despair and left, so the queue grew shorter.

When Hava went in to see the duty officer, who that morning happened to be Chief Inspector Orna Ben-Hamo, she put the box on the chair next to the one she sat down in and explained why she was there. She said that her mother had died – Orna expressed her condolences – and when the family had emptied out her flat they'd found the box with Emilia's things under a plastic chair on the balcony. Hava had contacted Emilia's employment agency to ask if she had relatives in Latvia to whom she should send the box, but they told her it would be best if she took it to the police. The belongings were not valuable but Hava thought that if Emilia had any relatives they would like to have them.

'Do you know what's inside? Did you look?' Orna asked.

'Yes, because we wanted to make sure everything in there really was hers and that there was nothing of Mother's that she'd taken. At first we didn't even know who the box belonged to.'

'Can you tell me what it contains?' Orna asked, even though the box was right there.

'Like I said, not much. Some clothes, notebooks, a few bits of homeware. I thought her family might want to have her clothes and the booklets.'

Chief Inspector Orna Ben-Hamo pulled out the summary of the Emilia Nodyeves investigation and read through it quickly to figure out what this was about. She told Hava, 'I'll give the box to the investigator in charge of the case and he'll decide what to do with it, all right? We don't deliver boxes overseas, but if the investigator decides he doesn't need it, he might contact you with the address of a relative there and you can send it yourself.'

Before she left, Hava asked if the police knew anything more about the circumstances surrounding Emilia's suicide, but Chief Inspector Ben-Hamo said she was not authorized to answer.

IN THE AFTERNOON, WHEN Orna finished her shift, she put Emilia's box in her office so that she could give it to the young detective the next morning. It was three o'clock, and she called her mother to find out how the girls were doing and let her know she'd be home in half an hour, if the traffic wasn't bad. Then she called her husband, but he wasn't available.

She made herself a cup of instant coffee with one teaspoon of brown sugar and grabbed two stale lemon wafers from the kitchenette because that's all there was. She stretched out her time alone in the office a while longer before going back to the girls. She had only returned to work the week before, after a four-month maternity leave, and was still readjusting to the station, the office, the uniform and the long stretches of sitting with citizens to hear their complaints. She wasn't supposed to be the duty officer that morning, but was called in at the last minute to replace an officer who'd torn his calf muscle running and couldn't come to work. The last case she'd worked before giving birth had to do with several similar incidents of identity theft used to open bank accounts, but it was transferred to a national unit while she was on leave, and she didn't even know if there'd been any new developments in it.

She glanced in Emilia's box, out of curiosity. She had a cardboard box, too, where she kept documents and certificates from secondary school and college, and even a plastic bag with love letters from old boyfriends. It was stored on the top shelf of the utility cupboard outside the bathroom, next to the gas masks. From reading the file, she'd understood that there probably wouldn't be anyone to send Emilia's belongings to, because no relatives had been located overseas. The open questions that Inspector A. had added to the file interested her, and she wasn't sure why he'd summed it up as a closed case: *Who was she sending money to in Latvia? Why was she planning to go to Riga if she was so afraid of being sent back there?*

In Emilia's box there were a few T-shirts, mostly grey, a book that looked like the Bible in Russian, a thin white curtain folded up like a prayer shawl, a towel, a green tablecloth and a glass vase. There were also a couple of pamphlets, old newspapers and one notebook, which was what Hava had called 'the booklets'.

Orna did not open the notebook because she was in a hurry to pick up Roni from nursery school and Naomi from school, and take over from her mother, who'd been with the baby, Danielle, since early morning.

In the afternoon the four of them went to the little neighbourhood park, and Roni almost got bitten by a dog that wasn't on its lead. Before she fell asleep that night, Orna thought about Emilia's dead face from the photograph in the file, and when she woke up in the middle of the night to feed Danielle she remembered the box. In the morning, before sending it on, she opened it again, without quite knowing why.

On the first page of the notebook were all the characters of the Hebrew alphabet, handwritten in one long column, and next to them in a different colour were the Latin characters that made the corresponding sounds. On the second page were lists of words: first the Hebrew, then a Latin transliteration, and finally the meaning.

The handwriting was an older man's or woman's, not a native Hebrew speaker, and the letters trembled on the page. Not all the words were easy to make out, but because they were simple, Orna was able to read them after some effort: 'אבא – ABA – father'; 'אמא – IMA – mother'; מים – MAYIM – water'; כוס – KOS – glass'; 'אוכל – OCHEL – food'; 'תרופה – TRUFA – medicine.'

After a few pages full of columns, there were some blank pages, and then the handwriting changed and so did the type of words. Instead of the neat columns there were single words, only in Hebrew, written in pencil, in large handwriting that drew the letters as pictures rather than writing them, the way her daughter Naomi did; she had started school in September.

Some pages contained only one word. For example, *mapah* – tablecloth, or *yetziah* – exit, *koma* – floor, *knesiyah* – church. Other pages had whole lines in Hebrew, almost a conversation, and next to them what looked like their translation into a language Orna did not recognize:

'Can you meet this evening?'

'When can I meet you? I miss your smell, Emilia.'

'I think about you more and more.'

There were some names in the notebook too. The name *Tadeusz* was written several times very carefully, in wide, round letters. There was also *Emilia*, drawn in various sizes, and *Nachum* and *Gil*. Since Orna already knew a little about Emilia's life, she could read the names like a story: 'Adina' was the old lady Emilia had cared for, 'Hava' was her daughter,' 'Gil' must have been the lawyer who had helped her and whose flat she'd cleaned. 'Nachum' was the old man she took care of for two years when she first came to Israel. 'Tadeusz' was the priest she used to talk with every Sunday, who had insisted when he was questioned that Emilia could not have committed suicide.

On one of the last pages in the notebook, Orna found her own first name.

7

SHE WILL TELL HIM that it's not realistic to just flit off overseas for a few days without any explanation. He will ask why, and she will say she can't leave her husband alone with the girls for a whole weekend and there's no one to help out. His mother is useless, and her parents are no longer alive. Besides, she will add, what reason could she give her husband for wanting to go? She can't tell him she's going away on her own to rest or let loose because it's unlike her and her husband knows that. She can't say she's going with a friend because even if she had the courage to go with Gil, she wouldn't tell any of her friends and ask them to lie for her. She'd be too scared of being found out.

She will tell Gil to drop it and he will. 'We'll have to make do with coffee and our correspondence,' she'll email him, 'even though I really would like to go away with you. You can't imagine how long it's been since I've had two days to myself.'

For a few days they will only email and meet at the café every morning and Gil will not propose anything beyond that, but after a while his emails will become seductive, pleading, bursting with desire. He will say that he sits in his office with clients and thinks about her, about things she told him that morning, and that if she asked him to, he would be willing to break up his marriage and leave his wife. Five minutes later he will send her another message that says, 'I'm sorry, delete the last message. I know it's not what you're after and I didn't mean to stress you out. I'm waiting for you patiently, you know exactly where, and if one day you want more than we have now (and we have a lot) I'll still be there.'

APRIL WILL ARRIVE, THE same month when the relationship between him and Orna had begun. There is a long school holiday over Passover, and Ella will explain that she won't be at the café much because the girls will be at home and the nanny is taking time off. He will say that he won't be there either because he's going to Poland and Bulgaria for a few days.

The glass walls that sheltered the café deck since November will be removed, and now that the deck is exposed to the street, they will move into the little indoor space, where the air conditioning will run all day. Outside, the first spring heatwaves will hit, the blue air will be dry and sandy and fragrant with blossoms and people will shed their coats and start wearing T-shirts again, but Ella will wear a windbreaker or a thin denim jacket, even when they go outside to smoke in the sun. In Riga, though, it will be the coldest April on record: at the beginning of the month there will be ten days of snow, and the river will still be almost completely frozen.

Gil will invite her to his flat, which will be empty but expected to start filling up with summer tourists in May, and she will refuse. He will no longer mention going away together, but when he tells her about his upcoming work trip she will be the one who wants to know more. 'Are you going alone?' she will ask, and he'll say, 'What do you mean?'

'I mean, I assume I'm not the only married woman you ask to go away with you, am I? You told me you've done it before.' She will smile and Gil will pause before saying softly, 'Do you really think I'm seeing other women now?'

She will ask him not to be so sensitive. And she will apologize. And then she'll ask, 'But if we went away together, what would we do there? After all, you're going for work.' Gil will explain that he'd be in meetings sometimes, but the rest of the time they could walk around and spend time in the hotel without being afraid someone might see them. They would be completely relaxed, in a way they cannot be in Israel.

'But how would we do it at this end? Would we take a cab to the airport together?'

'I would go a day or two ahead of you to get my work done, so we'd have time together, and you would join me. And we wouldn't have to take the same flight. Do you know how many flights there are between Tel Aviv and Poland or Romania every day?'

She will listen to him seriously, as if now, after he has explained how the trip might proceed, she sees things differently. 'And there?'

'There what?'

'There, would we stay in the same hotel? Same room? Is that how it's usually done?'

He will ignore the last part of the question and tell her that it could be the same hotel but it could also be adjacent ones. There's no shortage of hotels in Bucharest, or in Warsaw, and it's all up to her. But why wouldn't they stay in the same room? It's not like anyone knows them there.

'Do you have pictures? I'm curious. Show me what these hotels look like,' she will say, and he will reply that he doesn't have any pictures because he doesn't take pictures on work trips and he doesn't always stay in the same hotels, but he will promise to send her a link when he gets to work. 'It's a pity you're so afraid of him,' he will comment, and she will not respond. When he asks, 'What can he do to you, Ella? Tell me what he'll do?' she will say, 'Forget it. It's not him, I guess.' Gil will ask, 'Then who is it?' and she will say, 'Please, Gil. Forget it.'

That will be the last time they meet before his trip, and he will email her one picture while he's away: the old city of Warsaw in the evening hours, full of tourists and white horse-drawn carriages on the square outside a restored red palace. She will send back a message that he will notice was sent at 3 a.m.: 'I think I've found the perfect excuse to go away for two days. The paper, Gil! I have to do research for my seminar paper! Isn't it genius?'

*

WHEN HE GETS BACK he will think something has happened to her, as if she's made up her mind to conquer her fear even though she hasn't completely got over it and is not completely at peace with her decision. They will not be able to meet in the café because it will still be the school holidays. Instead, they will meet for the first time at night, in Yarkon Park. She will tell her husband she has to get some fresh air after being stuck at home with the girls all day, and he will tell Ruthi that he's going to the gym. They will walk along the river, at a safe distance from the streetlamps along its banks, and they will look for a secluded bench, but most of them will be taken. She will let him kiss her and touch her again, and when he lets go of her hand she will keep holding his. They will eat a bar of Belgian chocolate that he bought her at the airport because he thought she'd prefer a consumable gift, and she will tell him that she explained to her husband that while she was writing her seminar paper she'd come across a key document in the archives in Poland and she had to see it because it might be an important discovery. Her husband had suggested they all go together – he could take some time off and the girls could go, too, maybe in the summer, or earlier, on Shavuot holiday – but she'd insisted she had to go alone: she'd be working the whole time and it would be a quick trip. 'I haven't told him I'm definitely going yet, but I think he's okay with it.'

They will only be able to spend an hour at the park, at the end of which she will tell him she's almost positive she wants to go.

'But how did you suddenly decide? What happened?' he will ask, and when she says, 'I can't keep living in fear. I have nothing to be afraid of,' he will put his arm around her shoulder and say, 'Finally.'

They will agree that Gil will find out when his next work trip is and let her know. The next day, he will write that he has to be in Bucharest the following week for just over twenty-four hours, and after that they can stay on for two or three days in Warsaw or Krakow.

She will write back: 'Next week? Isn't that too soon? That's a little stressful for me. Can't you put it off?' He will answer that he can postpone his meetings for a few days if she promises to come with him.

She will not give him a final answer that day, and the next day she will not be at the café, and when Gil waits for her there he will think something might have happened, maybe even that her husband has found their correspondence. But when he gets to the office he will find two emails from her. The first will say: 'I'm coming. Weekend after next. We can leave on the thirtieth of April and come back on Sunday. But I don't know how often I'll come to the café until then and if it's a good idea for us to correspond.' In the second email, which he will accidentally read first, she will write her full name in English and her passport number, and that same day he will book tickets for them both.

8

THE HANDSOME YOUNG DETECTIVE had no objection to transferring Emilia's suicide case to Orna Ben-Hamo. He couldn't understand what she saw in it, and anyway he was busy with a series of intentional acts of sabotage on construction sites. He secretly regretted caving in to the pressure applied by HR to join Tel Aviv South Precinct instead of insisting on being assigned to one of the national investigation units, as he'd wanted and as his father thought he should be. Every time he drove his red Renault Clio Turbo into the building's underground parking early in the morning, he thought about the moment when he would go home in the evening.

Orna was summoned to speak with Commander Ilana Liss, who oversaw the Tel Aviv District's Investigation and Intelligence Branch, on the third floor of the police building on Salameh Street. She tried to explain to Commander Liss why she was not convinced that Emilia had committed suicide, as Inspector A. had presumed: 'We have the testimony of the priest, who was the closest person to her. He told us plainly that he didn't think she committed suicide. She was a devout Catholic, and apparently suicide is a transgression for them. Secondly, she was just about to go to Riga, either on holiday or on a trip that she wasn't going to come back from, we're not exactly sure. Why would she kill herself here a few days before that? It doesn't make sense. And there are also all sorts of toxicology reports that can't be done now, like those for date-rape drugs, but the fact that they weren't done at the time is very strange.'

Commander Liss asked if Orna minded if she smoked. She was already deep into her cancer treatments and these were her last few weeks on the job, although she didn't yet know that. Orna nodded and said, 'Maybe I'll even bum one off you.' They had hardly worked together before, because Commander Liss had been appointed to her position less than a year ago, after overseeing investigations and intelligence at Ayalon Precinct, and a few months after that Orna had gone on maternity leave. This meant that she could not read the expressions of the woman who was supposed to decide if it was worth pursuing the case. Orna added, 'But most important are the findings. Or rather, what we didn't find on the night she supposedly committed suicide. I don't understand how Inspector A. could have determined that she committed suicide outside, in the yard of a building near the central bus station, two hundred metres from our station, when no one saw her do it or saw her before. We know she left the nursing home in Bat Yam that morning, so all day long and all night she walked around that area and not a single camera picked her up? No one noticed a woman in such an unstable state? Besides, have you ever seen anyone commit suicide by covering their own head with a plastic bag?'

Ilana Liss put her lit cigarette in the ashtray. In her twenty-five years on the police force she'd seen every possible death, every imaginable form of cruelty – to oneself and to others. But she didn't want to say that to Orna, whose enthusiasm somehow reminded her of herself fifteen or twenty years ago, when she was taking her first steps in the Jerusalem district. She was living with her husband in an old stone house with a garden at the time, in a village outside the city, surrounded by pine trees that gave off a sharp smell of life every time it rained.

Inspector A. had thought all that was left to do on the Emilia Nodyeves case was to patiently await answers from the Riga police and then close the case, but Orna wasn't willing to give up. 'What did you tell me on the phone about the box someone brought in? I didn't follow,' Ilana said.

'I'm not so sure about the box, but there's something there I want to look into. It's one of the leads I'm pursuing at this point.' She told Ilana that in Emilia Nodyeves's notebook, which she'd found in the box, there was something apparently written in Emilia's handwriting, relating to the suicide of another woman, a resident of Holon named Orna Azran, who was found dead in a hotel room in Romania four years ago. 'It looks like a newspaper story that she copied, I'm not sure why.'

'What do you mean, copied?'

'She seems to have copied down all sorts of things.'

'Like what?'

'Sentences, fragments from all kinds of places. I'm not entirely sure where they're from.'

There was one piece that appeared repeatedly in the notebook that Orna was, in fact, sure about, but she didn't want to mention it to Ilana. It was the story Emilia had copied down several times from the church brochure, which was also in her box, about a woman named Tabitha or Tsivia who'd died in Jaffa and was resurrected. Orna preferred to keep that from Ilana because she was afraid it might reinforce Ilana's assumption that Emilia had been distraught and perhaps had even committed suicide because she thought she would be resurrected.

'Are we sure this notebook belongs to her?'

'Yes. That's how it seems. It looks like a notebook for studying Hebrew that she made or someone made for her. The story about the suicide of this Israeli woman is one of two passages she copied from a newspaper, and I'm not sure how she did that, because based on what I found out, Orna Azran's suicide and that story's publication in the paper happened before Emilia Nodyeves came to Israel.'

Ilana Liss put out her cigarette and got up to open the window and air the room. Every movement was hard, especially sitting down in the black executive chair, where three soft cushions had been placed on the leather seat. She tried to hide her pain. 'But why do you think this casts doubt on the Latvian woman's suicide? That's what I don't understand. It's the opposite, isn't it? She found a newspaper somewhere and read a story about an Israeli woman who committed suicide in a foreign country, and that's what provoked her thoughts of committing suicide here, no?'

'That's what I thought at first, too, Ilana. And maybe you're right and that's what happened. But I checked out the Orna Azran story and I found that it was also an unusual suicide, by strangulation, but with an electric cable. And in her case, too, everyone who knew the woman said there was no chance she'd committed suicide and insisted it was murder, just like the priest in Emilia's case. Doesn't that strike you as odd? Two women, where everyone who knows them says there's no chance they killed themselves, and the personal diary of one of them contains the other one's name and story, even though they don't seem to have known each other? And she also had the name and address of a hotel in Romania in her notebook – granted, it's not the same hotel where Orna Azran committed suicide, but still, it's strange, isn't it?'

Ilana Liss's mobile phone vibrated on the desk and she glanced at it and hissed something, then turned it over. 'It sounds like it could be a coincidence,' she said. 'This suicide in Romania, is it something we investigated?'

'No, it wasn't investigated in Israel at all. The woman's relatives asked us to investigate because they refused to accept the Romanians' findings, but they were told the case was examined by the Bucharest police and was closed.'

A flash of pain ran through Ilana's back and she straightened up. Then she told Orna, 'I have no problem if you want to take the case and decide when and how to close it, but I don't really understand how you're going to investigate that Bucharest suicide from here.'

THE FIRST STAGE WAS to demand all the details known to the Romanian police about Orna Azran's death and get the file translated into Hebrew. She found a translator, a native of Czernowitz who lived in Haifa, and after talking to him on the phone she was sure it would be weeks until he sent her the file: he was seventy-eight years old and wanted the documents faxed to him because he didn't do well with computers. But by noon the next day he'd already faxed her back the translation. Orna asked her mother to stay with the girls for an extra two hours and came home after six. She read the materials twice over and immediately started making phone calls.

For the time being, she was unable to speak with the Romanian witnesses, most of whom were hotel employees at the Trianon, where Orna had been found. But she did manage to talk to the Israeli witnesses, Orna's friends and relatives. The next day she sat at her desk opposite a short, thin man with long hair tied back in a ponytail, and if not for his facial expressions and smell, you might not have recognized him as Ronen, because of the intervening years and how grey his hair had gone. She asked if he was Orna's husband and he accidentally said yes, then clarified that he was her ex-husband. When she asked when they'd divorced and why he was named as her husband in the Romanian police files, Ronen said they'd divorced a year before the murder, but he might have introduced himself to the Romanian police as her husband to pressure them and so 'They would know that Orna wasn't alone, that she had family behind her who wouldn't let them neglect the case.'

On the desk he put down his light brown leather wallet, phone and a big bunch of keys that had been in his back pocket. He asked Orna why she'd asked him in, and she evaded the truth and said the family's repeated requests that the Israeli police look into the case were being reconsidered.

'It's about time. So what do you need from me?'

Orna pretended she wasn't even sure there was anything to investigate. 'To tell you the truth, I read your request, and the file, and I'm not all that convinced. I understand you had a difficult divorce, and that you left Israel and then came back and wanted to take her son away. That seems to me like a background that pretty much justifies what she did. So how about you explain to me why you don't think it was suicide?'

'Because Orna did not kill herself. She wouldn't have killed herself. So what if we had a difficult divorce? Of course she had difficulties, everyone has difficulties, but she was happy overall, and she would not have left Eran alone. Never. She would never have left Eran.'

'Eran is your son?'

'Eran is our son. She wouldn't have left him for a day, so she definitely wouldn't have committed suicide. Also, I didn't come back to take Eran away from Orna, as you put it. I just came to see him.'

'Then explain to me why she went to Romania.'

'What do you mean, why?'

'Why did she go without Eran? You said she wouldn't have left her son for a day, so how come she went away for a few days without him? Maybe she wanted to get away from him so she could do it?'

Ronen was wearing the faded red T-shirt that used to be Orna's favourite. His trousers were new. He was unshaven and the stubble on his narrow face was grey. His brown boots were bulky and very dusty. 'I don't know why she went there. Honestly. That's something to look into, and I don't think anyone did. Maybe she went because Eran was with me for a few days on the moshav, so she was able to get some rest. But to leave him for ever? Not a chance.'

When Orna asked what he thought had happened to her, Ronen said he had no idea but he was positive someone had killed her and she hadn't killed herself. The Romanian investigation had determined that no witnesses had seen Orna with anyone else from the moment she'd arrived at the hotel, and no one other than her had been seen going in or out of her room. But there were no cameras in the hotel corridors, and of course none in the rooms either.

'Forgive me for asking,' Orna said cautiously, 'but perhaps it's convenient for you to believe that? It could be that one of the reasons for her suicide was the state of things between you, the divorce and the fight over the boy, no? Isn't it possible that you're saying this out of guilt?'

'Of course I have guilt. I have endless guilt. But that's not why I'm saying this. I'm saying it because I know Orna didn't kill herself.'

'And the goodbye message she sent your son?' Orna read from the translation: 'Orna wrote explicitly that she wanted to die and couldn't keep on living after what had happened, didn't she?'

Ronen snapped: 'But that's just it – why would she write something like that to Eran? Would you write something like that to your son if you were about to commit suicide? And it wasn't true, anyway. When he talked to her on the phone that day she looked fine, and she told him she'd bought him presents, which they found in her room. So why would she say something like that to him? And where's her phone? How come the Romanians didn't find it? She sent a goodbye message from her phone and committed suicide and her phone disappeared?'

Orna explained that the Bucharest police had assumed the phone was stolen by the hotel cleaner who'd found the body, but she herself found that explanation unconvincing. One of the veteran employees of the Trianon was arrested a few weeks later on suspicion of stealing phones, jewellery and cash from hotel guests for years. He was questioned about possible involvement in Orna Azran's death, but denied stealing her phone, and according to hotel records he hadn't been at work on the day of her death.

She started asking Ronen different questions, shorter ones, and her tone was softer. 'Do you happen to know if she went away with someone? Anyone she might have gone away with?'

He said he didn't.

'Do you know if she was in a relationship with another man? Here or abroad? Do you think Orna was a woman who could have gone out to a bar or a restaurant, let's say overseas, met a man and gone back with him to her hotel?'

He said he didn't think so.

'Did she ever mention a man named Tadeusz to you?'

'Tadeusz?'

'Yes.'

'No.'

'How about Nachum? Or Gil?'

'No. But why are you asking me about these names?'

'Do you know if Orna happened to know a woman named Emilia in Israel? A Latvian woman named Emilia Nodyeves?'

She kept trying, and Ronen kept saying no. When she asked where Eran lived now, he said, 'With me,' and she asked, 'In India? I understand that's where you live.'

'I never lived in India. We lived in Nepal, but we came back to Israel and now we live in Holon. I didn't want Eran to have to move to a different country after everything that happened.'

Orna said she was also from Holon and asked where they lived. But they lived at opposite ends of town.

'And it's just the two of you here?'

'No. We're here with my second wife and her kids. Our kids. And Eran.'

With Ruth and Kurt and Thomas and Peter and Julia. And the baby, Lynne, who was born in Israel two months after they'd arrived. And Eran lived with them now. Julia was twelve and in the past year she'd sprung up and become almost as tall as her two older brothers, a head taller than Eran. She and Eran still shared a room, but they no longer got dressed in front of each other and they talked less before they fell asleep.

Orna debated briefly, then asked Ronen, 'Do you think I could talk to Eran?'

'I don't know. I'm not sure it would be good to take him back to all that. Can I consult with his therapist? He might have some advice.'

'Of course. You can call him now. And it's all right with me if he wants to be present for the conversation.'

'But why do you need to talk to him at all? What do you think he can tell you?'

She wasn't sure what to answer, because she couldn't say that she simply knew she had to see Eran.

9

THREE DAYS BEFORE THEY are supposed to go away together, an almost identical story will run in the crime sections of the two major dailies. The headline in *Israel Today* will be: 'Romanian Police Reopens Case of Israeli Woman's Death', and in *Yediot*: 'Was Bucharest Hotel Death a Murder Staged as Suicide?' Both stories will run in the inside pages, not particularly prominently.

The stories themselves will explain that, following new information obtained by the Bucharest police in recent weeks, they have reopened the investigation into the death of Orna Azran, a thirty-eight-year-old divorcée with one son who was found dead in a hotel room in the Romanian capital. New testimony from a front-desk employee, which was apparently overlooked previously, led Bucharest detectives to widen the scope of their search and collect additional testimonies indicating that, in the hours prior to her death, Azran had been seen with an unknown man. The Romanian police estimated that the anonymous man was local, but they were also looking into the possibility that he was an Israeli citizen. A sketch drawn in Bucharest, based on the new accounts as well as video footage, had been transferred via the embassy in Romania to the Israeli police.

The piece in *Israel Today* will also feature a small photograph of Orna – the same one that ran in the paper when her death was initially reported, which Emilia had found – and a black-and-white police sketch of the unknown man. At the end of the stories there will be a reminder of the details of the case, which had generated brief interest in the Israeli press a few years ago because of the family's insistence that Azran had not committed suicide but had been murdered, and because she had a young son.

SHE WILL PHOTOGRAPH THE story on her phone and send it to Gil. Under the picture she will write: 'Hey, this isn't you, is it? Should I be scared?' A few minutes later she will send him another message: 'Aren't you coming to the café today? Fleeing the law?' The face of the man in the police sketch, even though it will be a general outline that lacks precision or detail, will broadly resemble Gil's familiar face: round, too wide, fair eyes and a relatively full head of hair.

He will not answer her all day, so she will send him another message in the evening: 'That was a joke, in case you didn't know. I didn't mean to annoy you and I hope that's not what's happened. It was just the similarity in the picture and the trip to Bucharest, you understand, right? I thought it was funny. Anyway, you look better in real life. Less Romanian. Are you packing yet? Because I am, at least in my mind.' But that same night Gil will cancel the trip. First he will write tersely that something came up at work and he has to stay in Israel, and that he'll talk to her in a few days. She will send back a stunned, short email, after 3 a.m.: 'I don't believe you're cancelling now, after everything I went through for this. You're not really cancelling, are you?'

In the morning, at the café, she will write at length and more sharply: 'Are you serious, Gil? After I made up a whole story about going for research, with non-existent archives and meetings with imaginary researchers, you're calling it off? What could be so urgent at work? And at the weekend? I hope you understand that this was our only chance and there will not be another.' She will stay at the café until eleven o'clock, but will not write a word and will go out to smoke more frequently than usual. The next day she will come back and wait for Gil, but at ten o'clock she will shut down her laptop and take a cab home.

In the evening she will try a different tactic, a gentler one. She will email to ask if he can at least explain what happened and reassure her, tell her he's okay, that nothing's happened to him. He will not answer, and the next day she will not write and will not go to the café. At night she will do what she's never done before and try to call him from her phone, but his phone will be off and there will be no way to leave him a voicemail.

*

SHE WILL WRITE THE last email on Thursday night and Gil will read it on Friday. The subject line will be blank but the body of the message will say:

> So here's the deal: on Monday I sent you – as a total joke – a story from the paper about a woman in Romania, but because of what's happened since, I'm really not sure any more. *Is it you, Gil? Should I go to the police?* Are you somehow connected to that woman? Did you do something to her, and that's why you've disappeared? I'm going crazy because I feel like I'm imagining things, but on the other hand, what are you afraid of and why have you suddenly vanished??? You were so sure of yourself up until a few days ago, and you reassured me and made me believe it was so easy to go away together and that I had nothing to be afraid of. So what happened? If you don't write back and explain what really happened and why you disappeared on me, I think I really will do it in the end. I will tell the police I think it's you and that you were supposed to take me to Romania too. *Maybe even to the same hotel???* But I'm giving you the chance to explain yourself and spare me all the paranoia. And to think that at this very moment we should have been together for the first time! I have chills just thinking about it now. I deeply regret everything.

GIL WILL ANSWER WITHIN a few hours, but without saying a word about Orna or what happened in Romania or the news item.

He will say he's sorry, he had an income tax audit at work and he was busy all week running around to come up with documentation. He understands how disappointed she is, but he is even more disappointed and he promises to make it up to her. If she is still willing to go with him, he is sure they could find another date. When she doesn't answer his message, he will call her and she will answer in whispers from the bedroom. Gil will sound relaxed, and this time he will mention the newspaper story: 'You're not serious, are you? About what you said in your last message? I don't know which is more insulting, the fact that you thought I was a murderer or that you claim I look like the man in that picture.' She will not answer.

Then he will say he has to see her that weekend, and she'll whisper that there's no chance. He will insist and explain that he wants to apologize and get her forgiveness. She will say she can't talk any more and will hang up. He will call her again five minutes later and she will not answer, but he will keep calling and she will eventually answer from the bathroom and say she's begging him not to call now and they can meet at the café on Sunday.

But Gil can't wait. She will hear him say, 'You know, you're not the only one who can threaten. I can threaten you, too, can't I, Ella?'

She will not answer immediately. After a few seconds, she will say, 'What do you mean by that, Gil?'

'What would your husband say if he saw our emails? He'd probably be interested, wouldn't he? He'd also probably be interested to know why your research trip was really cancelled.'

She will sit down on the edge of the bathtub, shut her eyes for a moment, then open them. She will say she can meet him the next day, on Saturday, but only for half an hour. She will ask where he wants to meet, and he will suggest Yarkon Park.

'No, I'm sorry, I'm not hanging around with you in Yarkon Park on a Saturday afternoon.'

He will suggest they meet in his flat instead.

'Are you sure no one can see us there?' she will ask, and he will promise.

She will not have to write down the address because she will remember it.

When she arrives the next day, Gil will be waiting for her.

She will walk up the stairs in the dark, without switching the stairwell light on, and she will pause outside the door for a moment.

And then she will knock twice. And once more.

10

THE MEETING WITH ERAN took place at his therapist's office in Tel Aviv, two days after she met Ronen. The therapist had warned her over the phone that it would be difficult for Eran to talk about what had happened, and when Orna walked into the ground-floor office that looked on to a shady inner courtyard and stood in the doorway to the room where Eran was waiting, he said, 'If I feel it's necessary to stop the conversation, I suggest we do so and continue in a few days, all right?'

She immediately noticed Eran's resemblance to Ronen, because he wasn't a child any more. His eyes were black and direct like Ronen's the first time he'd looked at her. She shook Eran's hand and sat down on the wooden chair nearest to him. He was holding a mobile phone, and he slid it under his thigh on his red armchair. The therapist began by saying, 'So we've talked a little, Eran and I, about why you're here, but would you like to tell us some more?'

Orna said that due to the family's requests, she was looking into what had happened to Eran's mother again, and that she wanted to ask him a few questions. In the preliminary phone call with the therapist, she'd agreed not to raise Eran's hopes of hearing new information, the way his father sometimes did, and not to ask him questions about the divorce or the relationship between his parents, for now.

Orna took out a new cardboard file containing a list of topics she wanted to discuss with Eran. The protective presence of the therapist in the room was distracting and she wished she'd asked him not to be there, just as she'd insisted Ronen could not be in the room. He'd seated her opposite his own armchair, so that she was sitting next to Eran, rather than facing him as she would have liked. And she didn't feel that either of them needed the therapist there.

'You were the last person to talk to Mum that day, weren't you?' she began, even though she knew the answer from the reports.

THAT DAY'S CONVERSATION HAD been so short:

'How are you, my love?'

'I'm fine, Mum. Where are you?'

The last thing he asked you was if he could stay with Dad for a few more days, and you said no because you missed him.

'I WANTED YOU TO tell me a bit more about that phone conversation, because I don't know enough about it. Maybe you had the feeling something was wrong with how Mum was behaving or talking? Or she said something that you remember being surprised by? Or you saw something strange? You were on Skype, right?'

Eran looked at the therapist sitting in front of him, and then at the rug.

In the preliminary call, she'd asked the therapist if she could say in front of Eran that the assumption was that Orna had committed suicide, and he'd said yes. Eran knew, and most of their talks in recent years had been devoted to trying to convince him that she hadn't committed suicide because of him, or because he'd gone to stay with Ronen and his new family. That was why this meeting was so important. 'I don't know exactly what you're looking into,' the therapist had said, 'but if there's a chance that Orna did not commit suicide and something else happened to her, it could be very significant for Eran. That's why I thought we should have this talk.' He said the term they usually used was 'decided to die', rather than 'committed suicide', but Eran did sometimes say that 'Mum killed herself.'

'Maybe you remember if Mum seemed like she was in an ordinary mood, or if she looked different?' she asked.

Eran still didn't look at her when he said, 'Ordinary.'

'She was alone when you talked to her, right? You didn't see anyone else in her room?'

He hadn't.

'But did she mention that someone was with her? Or that she'd met someone there?'

He didn't know.

'Do you remember if, in the days before Mum's trip, she told you anything about her mood or about what she was going through? Did you maybe feel like she wasn't in a great mood?'

That was the only question she regretted. Eran had been nine at the time, and his father had come to visit after being absent for months, so what could he have sensed? She decided to change course: 'I want to ask you some different questions, some of which might sound silly or illogical, but that's how it goes sometimes in our work.'

The therapist smiled at both of them and said, 'Ours, too, right?'

'Do you remember if Mum ever talked about a woman called Emilia?'

No.

'Not an Israeli woman. Someone from overseas. Emilia Nodyeves?'

Eran shook his head.

'Or a man called Tadeusz?'

Eran still looked back and forth between the therapist and the rug. But when she asked, 'Do the names Gil or Nachum mean anything to you?' he looked up at her with his lovely eyes and nodded.

'Which one?'

Gil.

He said that was Mum's friend. She used to go to movies with him, and once they went to Jerusalem together. The therapist confirmed that Orna had mentioned a friend but he couldn't remember his name.

She still didn't know that this was the moment that would change her view of the investigation, not even when she asked Eran, 'Do you happen to remember Gil's last name?' He didn't. She wanted to hide the direction the investigation was going in from them, and the possible connection to Emilia's suicide, so she added, 'Because I'd be happy to talk to him and for him to tell me about Mum. Do you happen to remember anything she told you about him? Maybe where he worked?'

Eran didn't know. But when Orna asked, 'Do you remember if you ever saw him?' Eran immediately said that he'd seen him three times.

'Do you remember where? Or when?'

He remembered everything. He remembered meeting Gil by the box office at the cinema in Dizengoff Centre when they went to see *How to Train Your Dragon*. Gil was with another woman and two older girls, and Orna had introduced him to Eran. Another time he'd seen him from a distance, perhaps even before the time at the movies: Gil was in his car, he'd come to pick Mum up for the trip to Jerusalem, and Eran had watched from the window as she got into the car and waved goodbye.

The third time was hard for Eran to talk about, and the therapist tried to help him. He asked Eran if he was allowed to tell the policewoman, and when Eran nodded, the therapist said Eran had seen them at home. Orna hadn't told him that Gil was coming to visit, and she didn't know that Eran had woken up in the middle of the night and seen them asleep. Orna hadn't told him about it the next day either, and in fact they'd never discussed it. Eran told the therapist about it a few weeks after what happened to Orna in Romania, as an example of how Mum had kept secrets from him. The therapist had tried to convince him that maybe Orna wasn't hiding things but just hadn't had time to tell him, because it had happened a few days before she'd left.

Orna tensed up and asked if they knew exactly when this was, because she remembered from testimonies of relatives and friends that Orna was not in a relationship in the weeks before her trip to Romania.

'I might have it written down somewhere in my old notes,' the therapist said, but Eran had already leaned over to a blue backpack on the floor by the armchair and taken out the brown notebook that Orna had bought him for his birthday.

The date when Eran had seen Orna and Gil was written in the notebook. He told her the date, then leafed back and added, 'I also know what car he has, if that helps you find him and talk to him. He has a red Kia Sportage. I saw it when he came to take Mum to Jerusalem.'

ORNA CALLED COMMANDER ILANA Liss that night, after she got the second answer from the registration bureau.

The first one had been a disappointment. Attorney Gil Hamtzani, who had employed Emilia Nodyeves to clean his flat, owned two vehicles: a metallic-grey Toyota C-HR and a Volkswagen Polo. Orna doodled the same blue square over and over again on her page of questions, then asked the clerk: 'The C-HR is a new model Toyota, isn't it? That's not what I need. Can you tell me which cars he owned before those ones?'

When she called Ilana Liss she already knew with almost complete certainty that she wasn't wrong and that there was a connection between the deaths of Emilia and Orna.

‘So what are you saying?’ Ilana said. ‘I don’t get it. That he was responsible for both of their deaths?’

‘I don’t know yet. I do know that he apparently knew both of them, that he had a romantic relationship with Orna while he was married, and possibly with Emilia too. Or maybe with Emilia it was different and she somehow found out that he was connected to the first death, I don’t know yet. Maybe that explains the things she wrote in her notebook. What’s certain is that they both allegedly committed suicide under peculiar circumstances, without any of the people close to them understanding why, and that they both knew him.’

‘So explain to me the “allegedly”.’

‘Emilia definitely worked for Attorney Gil Hamtzani. That we know. And Orna was in a romantic relationship, right before her trip, with a man named Gil, who drove the exact same car Gil Hamtzani owned at the time. So I’m assuming it’s the same man, Ilana, but I have no definitive confirmation, and of course I’m still checking.’

Ilana Liss went into her study and lit a cigarette by the open window so that her husband and her kids wouldn’t smell the smoke. She wasn’t in uniform. She wore a thick, green cardigan over a black shirt and black sweatpants, and she watched the smoke she exhaled scatter into the night as she talked. ‘Checking what, exactly?’ she asked.

Orna said she wanted to find out where Gil Hamtzani was on the day Orna allegedly committed suicide – whether he was in Bucharest or in Israel – and where he was on the day Emilia’s body was found. She wanted to know more details about him, about his history, his relationships with women, but without questioning his family or immediate surroundings, so as not to arouse suspicion. In fact, she was still far from being convinced it was the same Gil, but she'd decided to move forward on that presumption, and when she was later asked why she'd acted that way, she could not explain it. She wanted to get records of Gil's phone calls and precise dates of when he'd left and entered Israel, and to file a request to listen in on his phone, at home and at work, even though it was still premature.

Only after Ilana Liss authorized her to start the procedure for opening a covert investigation did Orna tell her husband, Avner, about the case. He tried to listen attentively, even though he was tired, because he could see how upset she was. He turned the girls' reading lamp off and tucked them in and made two cups of coffee for him and Orna so that he could keep his eyes open. They sat in the kitchen while she told him about her breakthrough with Eran and the sense of urgency she'd felt since reading about Orna Azran in Emilia Nodyeves's notebook and had considered for the first time that the two cases were connected.

'If that turns out to be true, then it's really unbelievable that you figured it out,' said Avner, clearly impressed.

'I'm almost positive. And it's all thanks to her son, do you see? I wouldn't have been able to verify the connection without him.' She told him that since Hava Yashar had put Emilia's cardboard box in front of her that day, she'd felt something propelling her towards this case and it wouldn't let go. She'd never felt this way before, not even when she'd been involved in big cases.

'It's because of the maternity leave, isn't it?' Avner suggested. 'After four months at home you need this kind of action.'

'I don't think so. I feel that I was supposed to meet that boy, do you understand?'

But he didn't. And he managed to irritate her by saying that she'd always been that way, extremely driven to prove herself and get to the top, and that this case, if it turned out to be what she thought it was, was a chance for her to show everyone what she could do.

She stayed up long after he fell asleep. At 3 a.m. she woke up to feed Danielle and soothe Roni, who had woken up crying because she thought there was someone in the house. Even so, she got up before Avner did, when it was still dark outside. She made herself some sweet tea with lemon and drank it in the dining area by the closed window, which the rain was beating down on, before she made the girls breakfast and packed their lunches.

THE NEXT BREAKTHROUGH CAME five days later, when she decided to show Gil's neighbours the pictures of Orna and Emilia, without saying anything about their connection with him. She arrived shortly after ten o'clock, after making sure Gil and his wife had left for work. She went from door to door in their building, showing the pictures and asking if anyone had ever seen these women. Only when she got to the second floor did she realize she was in the wrong building: this was not where he took Orna, nor was it the flat Emilia had cleaned, based on the address she'd written in her notebook and the testimony Gil himself had given Inspector A. when he was first questioned.

The plain-clothes detective who accompanied her went up ahead into the correct building, in Givatayim, and knocked on Gil Hamtzani's door. No one answered, so she went from door to door, showing the pictures.

The neighbour across the hall didn't recognize Orna's photo, but when she saw Emilia's picture she said, 'Her I know. Definitely. She used to clean the flat across the way.'

Orna already knew that, but she did not know the things the neighbour told her next.

She asked the neighbour if she'd ever talked to Emilia, and she replied, 'Actually, yes. By chance. I knocked on the door while she was there and asked if she wanted to work for us, because the guy who cleaned our place was deported. She didn't want to.'

'Do you remember when the last time you saw her was?' Orna asked.

'The last time? No, I don't think so. A long time ago. Actually, I do remember seeing her come over in the evening once. And on a strange day – I think it was a Friday or Saturday, because I wondered what she was doing there, whether she'd come to clean at the weekend or if she was going in without him knowing, because he always left her the key in the fuse-box cupboard. I even thought of calling to ask Gil if she was supposed to be there, but I don't have his number, and also I didn't want to get her into trouble. Did something happen to her?'

The neighbour couldn't say which Friday or Saturday she'd seen Emilia at Gil's in the evening, but Orna had no doubt that it was the day before her body was found on Ha'Galil Street. It suddenly occurred to her that there might have been, or still be, other women. 'Have you seen another woman come here since then?'

The neighbour looked at her as if she couldn't understand the question. 'You mean a woman who comes to clean?'

'To clean, or maybe someone else who comes here a lot.'

'They refurbished the apartment a few months ago, and I don't think anyone lives there regularly. I think they rent it out short-term to tourists, and it's empty a lot of the time. But I don't understand who you're looking for. Is it this woman? I think I even remember her name: Emilia, isn't it?'

'Never mind, I'll ask them.' She thanked the neighbour and turned around to knock on Gil's door, even though she knew he wasn't there. She waited until the neighbour went back inside. Despite the refurbishment, the door was the same old brown wooden door that still had no name on it, just the same slightly rusted copper number: 3.

11

HE WILL OPEN THE door with a grave expression, looking pale and tense, as if he hasn't slept for days. He will not say a word when he sees her, and she will stand there, awkward and jumpy, in the doorway to the almost-bare flat, without knowing where she is supposed to go and where he wants them to talk.

On the kitchen table, which will be the same table, there will be the embroidered tablecloth that Emilia bought, and the wicker basket, with no fruit. A glass mug of steaming water will be on the table, and Gil will point to it and ask what she wants to drink. When she says she doesn't want anything, he will say, 'I've made some for myself and I'll make you some too. Regular tea with lemon and sugar, is that okay?'

She will still be able to get up and run, but she will remain seated. When he puts the tea on the table and sits down next to her she will say pointedly, 'Can you explain why you threatened me?'

Gil will look almost surprised. 'When did I threaten you?'

She will answer, 'What do you mean? Didn't you threaten to show my husband our emails and tell him about the trip?'

'You know I wouldn't do that,' he will say. 'It was the only way to get you to meet me.'

ALL THE ROOMS WILL have a faint smell of paint, glue and dampness, which will have replaced the odour of cigarette smoke from the Chinese labourers that permeated it during the refurbishment. The kitchen, bathroom and toilet will be new, and the other rooms will have parquet flooring. The little bedrooms that Emilia cleaned thoroughly, as though they were going to be hers, will be furnished with things he bought alone at Ikea. The wooden wardrobe in the big bedroom will have been replaced by a new one, with sliding glass doors. In the window, with a view of the garden where Emilia used to see Nachum, and where Orna loved to look at the tall trees swaying against the house, an electric blind will have replaced the old one, and the copper bell that hung from the frame will be gone. There will be a suitcase containing clothes, toiletries, ten thousand shekels in cash and an ultra-Orthodox Jew's outfit: black coat, black felt hat, wig purchased that week in Bnei Brak. In one of the drawers he will have two passports with his picture but different names, and two plane tickets to different destinations that he does not yet know if he will use.

She will not drink the tea Gil made her but will wrap her hand around the mug, and when he tries to touch her she will pull back and not let him. He will say, 'I'm sorry I cancelled the trip, but I really had no choice. Won't you forgive me? Everything was going so well for us.' She will say, 'Gil, you have to understand – I don't believe you any more. Not a single word. Not just because of the trip but because of the threats. I came here to ask you for something, and then I'm leaving. I want you to listen to me for a second and be rational, so that we can end this respectably, okay?' And he will say, 'Of course. Whatever you want.'

It will still not be too late for her to get out. It will be early evening, only just getting dark. Outside it will be unusually quiet for a Saturday night, with no cars passing by.

'I don't believe you any more. It's that simple, and we have nothing more to talk about. I don't want to know why you came on to me and why you wanted me to go away with you and why you cancelled at the last minute and what you actually wanted from me. I don't want to know who you are or what you want. Whether you're a lawyer or not, whether you're married or not. I'm just scared of you now and of what you could do to my life. Are you listening to me? So I'm asking you to delete my phone number and the text messages and emails I sent you, and for us to cut off this relationship. I promise to delete your messages and not make contact with you again. Do you agree?'

He will look at her for a moment and seem to be deliberating, but he will say, 'Yes, I agree. Even though it doesn't make me happy. I had no intention of hurting you.'

'So you're deleting everything? Not tomorrow but now? While I'm here, and you'll show me?'

'If that's what you want, then yes. I don't have my work computer here, but I have the phone.' He will take a phone she does not recognize out of his pocket and then put it back and take out the phone she remembers. He will put it on the table. 'But I want to know: did you really think I was the man from the newspaper picture? Did you think I did something to that woman? And that I was planning to hurt you too?'

She will say, 'I don't know. I didn't know what to think. It was a coincidence, that picture, but then you suddenly cancelled without any explanation. The whole thing stressed me out. It could be that I was just really panicked by the idea of the trip, and the way you behaved didn't exactly help.'

'Did you tell anyone about it?'

'About what?'

'About the picture. The newspaper.'

'Who would I tell? Who could I tell? No one knows about me and you. And I would like it to stay that way.'

'Me too.'

But instead of dropping the subject, she will go on: 'Why were you so hurt, can you explain that? If you have nothing to do with that story, why were you so spooked by what I wrote? That's what I still can't understand. Are you sure you didn't cancel the trip because I hurt your feelings?'

*

THE BLINDS IN THE living room will be slightly open, but the thick glass panes will be shut and that is why the flat will be so silent. Everything will be closed up in the bedroom, too, and it will be completely dark. Gil will lock the front door from inside when she goes to the toilet, and for the rest of their conversation the key will be in his pocket. Before she arrives, he will have covered the bed with an old grey sheet he doesn't need.

He will get up from the kitchen table and come back with a glass of water and a little plastic bag that he will put down by the table leg. Only when he asks, 'And if I do have something to do with the woman in Romania, then…?' will it be clear that he has made up his mind what to do.

There will be no fear on her face when she looks at him, only surprise. 'Then what? What if you do? I don't understand.'

'That doesn't mean I was planning to hurt you the same way, you see?'

She will tense up, and he will see it. When she stands up and says she wants to leave, he will tell her she can't leave because the door is locked and he has the key. He will grab her hand and she will say, 'Gil, stop it, let me go. I have to get home and you're scaring me again.' But her voice will not sound panicked.

Without answering her, he will try to block her mouth with his hand, still without the gloves that will be in the plastic bag by the table, but he won't be able to. Only then will she suddenly say, in a changed voice, 'Don't touch me. I'm wearing a wire and there are police officers outside and they will come in to arrest you now, and you will not resist. It's over.'

When Gil says, 'Nice try,' she will say, 'It's over, Gil. I'm telling you, I'm a police officer and you're under arrest. I suggest you not make a single move now.'

He still will not believe her.

Not even when the blue lights from outside filter through the slats of the blinds, and the silence up and down the street gives way to police sirens, and the first thuds of heavy iron mallets are heard pounding on the door.

12

THE FIRST STAGE OF the covert investigation conducted by Chief Inspector Orna Ben-Hamo lasted about six weeks, from the beginning of January to mid-February, during which time she gathered all the information she was able to obtain on Gil without questioning his family and friends.

She knew he was born in May 1962, in Tel Aviv, and that he had served as an adjustment in the army. He'd studied law at Tel Aviv University, clerked at the magistrates' court in Ramleh and passed the Bar in 1988. In 1991 he married Ruth Levanon, whose family owned a lot of land in the Tel Aviv area, and her parents gave them the flat she'd grown up in, in Givatayim. They had two daughters, one of whom was now in the army. Gil's father, whom Emilia had cared for, had died more than two years ago, and his mother, who had time to testify to Inspector A., the first detective on the case, had died a few months ago. Gil had worked for a large employment agency until, in 2002, he started his own law firm, using some money from his father-in-law. She knew part of his work involved frequent trips to Eastern Europe, mostly because he was now managing real-estate investments there. He might also be involved in other businesses. She knew he'd been in Bucharest during the time of Orna Azran's visit, but she also knew he would be able to claim he was there at least once a month and that it was a coincidence that they'd been there at the same time, even if he did not deny that they had previously been in touch. She found out from the income-tax authorities and the Ministry of the Interior that Gil had never been suspected of tax evasion or failure to report income, and that his work with the Population and Immigration Authority had also never been under scrutiny. However, one of his clients was an Israeli contact who had been suspected of importing illegal workers from Eastern Europe, and Orna briefly considered using that to get Gil into the interrogation room so she could question him. But she had to abandon the idea. Gil's wife, Ruth Levanon-Hamtzani, was a partner in one of the largest law firms in Israel, which was another reason to be very cautious in the investigation.

At the beginning of February she had a series of disappointments. She tried to obtain evidence that Gil had booked Orna Azran's flight to Bucharest and her hotel room, but it was too long ago and the transactions were no longer available. Records of phone calls also revealed nothing, because he'd used a second phone with a prepaid SIM card. She thought if she could get concrete evidence of his being romantically involved with Orna around the time of her trip, and perhaps with Emilia, too, it would be enough to move to an open investigation, try to break him in the interrogation room and gather evidence from relatives and friends. But she didn't want to take that risk, and had no real evidence that Gil's relationships with Orna and Emilia had continued up until the time of their deaths. There was only the testimony of Eran, who had seen Gil in their home, and of the neighbour who'd seen Emilia enter Gil's flat on a Friday or Saturday. And both of them could be disputed.

There were days when she thought of throwing in the towel. Other cases came in and at some point she was asked to join an intra-precinct investigation team working on a scheme targeting elderly people around the country, and she wondered if she shouldn't put Orna and Emilia's deaths aside, if only temporarily. Emilia had no relatives pressuring her to keep investigating, and when Ronen called every few days to ask if there was any progress, she could tell him the investigation was stuck. None of her supervisors thought there was any point in continuing, but still she felt she couldn't give up: something was driving her. It wasn't the action, as Avner had said when they'd first talked about the case, not her drive to be the best or anything else about her soul or her life, or at least that was how she felt. It was the fact, which she had not confessed to anyone, that she thought she could see Emilia, and that every so often she found herself driving down Balfour Street in Bat Yam or past the nursing home where Emilia had worked, or smoking a cigarette on the square outside the church in Old Jaffa where Emilia had sat on her last day. This had never happened to her before.

That was where she first had the idea of following him. She was too impatient to wait and she called Ilana Liss from the church square.

Ilana was sceptical. 'What exactly is that going to achieve? You suspect he's involved in crimes committed years ago. He's not going to do anything connected to that now, certainly not unless we make him.'

Orna wasn't sure what it would achieve. She wanted to observe him from up close. She also thought he might be in touch with other women, and that perhaps they were in danger. That was what finally persuaded Ilana. A detective unit followed Gil for three rainy days in late February and didn't come up with much. He left for his office every morning and came home in the afternoon or early evening. Once he went on a bike ride with a group in Yarkon Park and once to the gym. He didn't visit his rental flat in Givatayim and didn't meet any woman who wasn't his wife. On two of the three mornings, he stopped on the way to work at a café near his home in Givatayim.

Ilana Liss would not authorize Orna to try to make contact with him or monitor him herself, so one morning she simply went to the café, without telling anyone. She had never done anything like that before, but this time she had to. She brought her laptop and pretended to work. She did not yet have a clear plan.

He didn't come to the café on the first morning, or the second. But on the third he did. And he looked at her that first time. Until that moment he had been a person whose name she had read in the investigation files and had heard other people talking about, and now their eyes met. She knew it was him. But she still had no idea how she was going to catch him, and only after they made initial contact, on his initiative, did she tell Ilana Liss about him.

She knew Ilana would be furious, and she was, but she still tried to persuade her. 'He initiated the first contact, Ilana, not me,' she explained, 'so let me continue. If it doesn't work out, I'll send the case on.'

Ilana didn't understand. 'But continue what, exactly?'

That was not clear yet. Get closer to him and try to make him tell her something. Or try to develop a relationship with him and see if he followed a similar pattern.

Ilana gave her a week – with a list of conditions. The first was that they were not to meet anywhere except the café, and that there must always be a plain-clothes detective there. When she asked how their contact had been established, Orna told her the truth: 'I somehow realized what would make him talk to me. Without planning anything. Based on the few details I knew about him, I guess. I had to explain what I was doing in the café every morning and why I had my laptop, and somehow I ended up with this story about Eastern Europe. I really did study history at college and I worked in the Museum of the Diaspora for a few months.'

She'd picked the name Ella without much thought. After their first cigarette together, she'd almost told him her name was Orna. Later it occurred to her that she might have come up with the name 'Ella' because of the famous Tel Aviv restaurant Orna & Ella.

EVERY DAY IN MARCH, after they met at the café, she went back to the station and wrote up a thorough report, which was Ilana's second condition. Several times, she conducted loud phone calls in the café and mentioned the phone number she was hoping Gil would call, and he did make a note of it. The fact that it was winter helped her – she could hide the recording device under her coat.

She did not tell Avner anything, not even when she met Gil for lunch in Jaffa and let him touch her and kiss her. She also left those details out of the report she wrote the next day. Thanks to the pictures of the women, which never left her, she imagined in those moments that she was Emilia or Orna and that was what helped her get through it. She said things to him that seconds before she hadn't known she was going to say, and if someone had asked her to explain how she'd come up with them or whether they were true, she would have preferred not to answer or think about it.

At first Gil disclosed nothing that could have moved the investigation forward, even though once in a while she tried to cautiously prod him in the right direction. When he mentioned the idea of going away together, she finally felt she was getting closer. At this point she was so focused on the case and on Gil that if she'd had to, she would have gone to Bucharest with him. But she knew Ilana Liss would never authorize that, and in their last conversation, before Ilana took the sick leave from which she never returned, they hatched the idea of taking advantage of his suggestion to go to Romania. They would make him organize the trip, to see if he would repeat his presumed behaviour patterns, find out which hotels he would book and how he would purchase the tickets, and then pressure him by publishing a semi-fictitious story in the papers and hope he would do something he hadn't planned to. The police sketch was drawn by Freddy Amsaleg in under an hour, based on a picture from the driver's licensing authority and Orna's input. When it worked and he asked her to come to his flat, she believed he might actually confess to the murders of Orna and Emilia before he tried to hurt her, but he didn't. In his interrogation, after the arrest, he claimed he hadn't tried to hurt her at all and denied any connection to the two deaths. His lawyer informed them that he would ask to rule out all investigation findings obtained through Orna, but the Tel Aviv District's deputy DA, who met her at court and complimented her on her work, said, 'This is just the beginning of the process, but even if he continues to deny everything, we have enough evidence to put him away.'

According to her prior agreement with Ilana, she never met Gil again. All subsequent questioning was conducted by other investigators, including the handsome young detective who now regretted not keeping the case, although he tried to hide that from Orna.

When she heard that the investigators were getting arrest warrants for Gil's wife and daughters, to pressure him, she assumed it would be over soon.

TWO DAYS AFTER THE arrest, on Monday, Orna didn't have to go to work because she had asked for the day off. She woke up before sunrise, as she did almost every morning that winter, for no reason and even if she'd gone to bed late.

It was still dark outside.

She didn't want to wake Avner, so she got out of bed and put on a sweatshirt. She made a cup of coffee, and when she opened the kitchen window the cold air blew in, along with the smell of rain and wet roads. Later, she dropped the girls off at school and nursery school, then went back home and tidied up, and at eleven her mother came to watch Danielle. She called Ronen and arranged to visit him at home that afternoon. Ruth opened the door, wearing a white knee-length *jellabiya*, and invited Orna to come in and sit down at the kitchen table. The kitchen was dirty, full of dishes with leftover pasta in tomato sauce and unwashed pots and pans. Ruth left her alone with Ronen, and she told him they'd caught the man who had apparently hurt Orna.

'What do you mean, apparently?' he asked.

'He hasn't confessed yet, but I can tell you with absolute certainty that he hurt her and that she did not commit suicide. It's the man she was going out with for a few months. The man Eran saw. He seems to have been the person she went to Romania with. I didn't update you sooner because the investigation was covert for a few weeks, but he was arrested yesterday.'

'But why did he do it? Did he explain why?'

She couldn't answer that, because Gil was still denying everything.

She asked if she could talk to Eran, and Ronen hesitated and said it might be best if he asked the therapist to be present for their conversation. She said that was no problem and she would wait. There was a picture on the fridge of Ronen and Ruth with their kids, including Eran, in the Golan Heights or maybe some other green mountainous area, all with sleeping bags rolled up in backpacks on their backs and heavy walking shoes. Eran was standing next to Julia, who had her hand on his shoulder. Below that picture was another one, which showed Eran on the Tel Baruch beach with Orna; it was a picture Ronen had taken on Eran's fourth birthday.

The therapist couldn't come, but he said it was fine with him if Orna talked to Eran in Ronen's presence. So the three of them sat in the kitchen, Ronen next to Eran with his hand on the back of his neck, and her opposite them.

She said to Eran, 'I want to tell you that we caught the man who hurt Mum. That means we know that Mum did not kill herself. Someone else hurt her. She was planning and hoping to come back to you, and this man prevented her from doing it. Do you understand?'

He covered his eyes so she would not see him crying.

'I also want to tell you that I think we were able to catch this man thanks to you,' she added. Ronen asked why she said that, and she said she would give them more details later. She didn't want to tell Eran now who the man who hurt his mother was, and how without the things he'd seen and written in his notebook, about Gil's car and the night he saw them in her bedroom, he would probably never have been caught. But she did say they would probably need to talk to the police again, and testify at the trial.

Ronen nodded. 'We'll do whatever we have to.'

She had two hours before she had to pick up the girls.

She could still smell Gil's cologne and feel the taste of his lips in her mouth. She called Avner to hear another voice, and when he answered and realized she was upset, he asked if something had happened and if she wanted him to come home early. She picked up voicemails from a few officers in the precinct who'd called to congratulate her, but unlike with previous cases, she did not feel she ought to be congratulated because she hadn't really done anything. The people who'd caught Gil were Eran and Ronen, who'd insisted that Orna couldn't have committed suicide, as well as Ilana Liss, who'd allowed her to keep investigating, even when she couldn't explain why. And Emilia. Someone should be notified that Emilia's murderer had been caught, too, not just Orna's. So she called Tadeusz, as it was thanks to his initial testimony that the first doubts had arisen in her mind. But Tadeusz's phone was off, and when she called the church and asked to speak to him, she was told he had left Israel because his mission here had ended and he'd been sent to Rome. Since there was no one she could tell about Emilia, she talked to her in her heart.

Her mother stayed for a while after she got home. Orna couldn't tell her much because the investigation was under a gagging order, but she promised to say more soon. When she was alone with the girls she felt the need to do something different with them, something they'd never done before, something she and they would always remember. But it was beyond her capacity that day, and the afternoon dragged on in her efforts to get organized. The girls didn't want to go to the beach to play in the sand and see the sunset, they only wanted to watch TV. And so at seven o'clock she found herself cooking eggs and peeling cucumbers for dinner, as she did every evening, while they spread ketchup all over the kitchen and themselves and tried to make their own cheese sandwiches.

With Avner there were actually some nice moments of intimacy in the evening, and she told him more than she'd thought she could.

Throughout that whole winter, Avner had known almost nothing of what she was going through, even though he did ask and did listen when she wanted to talk. She felt restless, as though she'd forgotten something in Gil's flat, and even though it was late, she checked her phone every few minutes to see if anyone had emailed or texted her. Inspector A. called to congratulate her, but Ilana Liss did not because she was in hospital.

About the meetings in the café, about the lunch in Jaffa, and the last meeting with Gil in his flat – she did not tell Avner. She simply said they'd trapped him by luring him into a romantic correspondence, and that she'd been instrumental in the arrest. While she talked about Gil she could see him before her, in the moments when he'd opened the door and when he'd put his hand on her shoulder. She got up so that Avner would not see her eyes, and when she came back to the living room with a bowl of nuts, she asked him about his work.

Even though she was exhausted, she couldn't force herself to fall asleep while Avner was still awake, the way she wanted to. She felt the hours ticking by and the night growing shorter.

When she was almost asleep, she heard Danielle cry and got up to make a bottle and feed her. Shortly after that, Roni woke up, too, as she did almost every night that winter, saying she was afraid there was someone in the house.

Orna stroked her soothingly, whispered that no one besides them was in the house, and when she heard her daughter's quiet, sleeping breaths, she went back to bed and shut her eyes. And this time, she managed to doze off, because you stayed with her all night to guard her sleep.